CLASH OF FLAMES

AN IAN DEX SUPERNATURAL THRILLER BOOK 7

JOHN P. LOGSDON

CHRISTOPHER P. YOUNG

This is a work of fiction. All of the characters, organizations, and events portrayed in this novel are either products of the author's imagination or are used fictitiously and are not to be construed as real. Any resemblance to actual events, locales, organizations, or persons, living or dead, is entirely coincidental.

Copyright © 2018 by John P. Logsdon & Christopher P. Young

All rights reserved, including the right to reproduce this book, or portions thereof, in any form.

Published by: Crimson Myth Press (www.CrimsonMyth.com)

Cover art: Jake Logsdon (www.JakeLogsdon.com)

Thanks to TEAM ASS!
***A**dvanced **S**tory **S**quad*

This is the first line of readers of the series. Their job is to help me keep things in check and also to make sure I'm not doing anything way off base in the various story locations!

(listed in alphabetical order by first name)

Adam Saunders-Pederick
Bennah Phelps
Debbie Tily
Hal Bass
Helen Saunders-Pederick
Jamie Gray
Jan Gray
John Debnam
Larry Diaz Tushman
Marie McCraney
Mike Helas
Natalie Fallon
Noah Sturdevant
Paulette Kilgore
Penny Campbell-Myhill
Sandy Lloyd
Scott Reid
Tehrene Hart

Thanks to Team DAMN
Demented And Magnificently Naughty

This crew is the second line of readers who get the final draft of the story, report any issues they find, and do their best to inflate my fragile ego.

(listed in alphabetical order by first name)

Adam Goldstein, Amy Robertson, Barbara Henninger, Beth Adams, Bethany Olsen, Bob Topping, Bonnie Dale Keck, Carmen Romano, Carolyn Fielding, Carolyn Jean Evans, David Botell, Dawn Blankenship, Denise King, Dorothy Phillips, Emma Porter, Helen Day, Jacky Oxley, Jim Stoltz, Jodie Stackowiak, Kathleen Portig, Kevin Frost, Laura Stoddart, Mark Brown, Mary Letton, MaryAnn Sims, Megan McBrien, Megan Thigpen, Michael Stivers, Myles Mary Cohen, Patricia Wellfare, Pete Sandry, Rob Hill, Ruth Nield, Sara Mason Branson, Scott Ackerman, Sharon Harradine, Stacey Stein, Stephen Bagwell, Steve Woofie Widner, Tony Dawson, Zak Klepek.

CHAPTER 1

Sleep wasn't easy to come by for those who worked in the Las Vegas Paranormal Police Department (PPD). First off, you worked nights, so you had to be comfortable sleeping during the day. Secondly, you were always on edge because you never knew when a member of the supernatural community might do something naughty to a normal. And third, you were hornier than the average person due to the genetic enhancements you got when you became a full cop.

Each officer was enhanced for their particular race. A vampire was quicker and more agile, a werewolf was stronger and faster, a mage could cast more spells without running out of juice, a pixie could throw dust or use more creative curse words, and so on. But they only got one increment on the level of horny.

I was different.

I was an amalgamite. That meant I'd gotten bits of vampire, werewolf, pixie, fae, werebear, and various other sprinkles in my system. So when I got my enhancements on the day of becoming a full cop in the PPD, I ended up getting a bunch of horny points. That, in turn, essentially made me the horniest guy on the planet.

I kept it in check most of the time, but it wasn't easy. There are a lot of hot chicks in Vegas, you know.

What made it worse was that I'd recently been bitten by a vampire whose venom unleashed *a lot* more of my powers.

For example, I used to be able to cast a simple illumination spell using my mage abilities.

That was it.

Nothing fancy.

Now, though, I could launch spells that the mages on my team drooled over. I could also pop out my fangs like a real vampire. I couldn't do that before. On top of that, I got faster, stronger, had more stamina, and was technically 'better' in every way than I was before that vampire bite.

Now, I know what you're thinking...

How could it possibly be *worse* that I had better powers?

Because my girlfriend, Rachel Cress, who also happened to be my partner on the force, had taken a real shine to my new demeanor.

She used to be the one who snarked at me all the time, called me an idiot, and had the upper hand in our relationship. But since that damn vampire shoved venom in my veins, I was loaded with angst and brooding. It turned out, this got Rachel's engine revving.

Where she once spent half the time staring at me with

crossed arms and a tapping foot, she now swooned over me...mostly. Now and then she'd break out of her Ian-is-yummy mindset and be her old self, but it wasn't like it used to be.

Okay, so now you're *really* confused.

How could it possibly be *worse* that I had better powers *and* my girlfriend swooned over me instead of calling me an idiot all the time?

Because we'd been having so much sex that I barely got any sleep!

I'll admit that this doesn't sound like the worst problem a guy could have, but I was the chief of the Las Vegas PPD. I needed to be on my toes at all times, and I needed to have my wits about me, too.

"Ian," Rachel said as I stood in the shower, letting the hot water do its best to revive me, "mind if I join you?"

Honestly, the woman had become more insatiable than me.

Me!

But I couldn't say no. It just wasn't in my DNA.

So I held out my arm, signaling for her to join me.

"*Now, we're talkin',*" said The Admiral, who happened to be my dick.

Yes, my dick spoke to me.

We have had many conversations over the years, in fact. It made it quite awkward to pleasure myself, but fortunately it was rare that I needed to do that anymore. These days, when I did give myself the old low-five, The Admiral and I had a strict no-talking rule that we followed.

To make things even more fun, Rachel could *also* hear

it when The Admiral spoke. I have even referred to her as "The cock whisperer." Crude, yes, but that's how my brain worked.

She smiled at The Admiral's enthusiasm, letting her robe drop as she stepped inside.

My condo had an open-style shower that could fit four people comfortably. Trust me, I know. That's what you got when you lived in a 3.5-million-dollar hedonistic hovel at The Martin in Las Vegas.

Within moments, our hands were all over each other.

I was tired, but when you had a woman as hot as Rachel pressing her nakedness against you while hot water rained down on your back, you tended to wake up.

Crash.

We both opened our eyes and looked at each other.

"What was that?" she asked.

"No idea," I replied, but I let my senses reach out through my property.

One of the many things I was gifted with as an amalgamite was the ability to know if there was anything out of place in my condo. It had saved my ass on many occasions, in fact. Bad guys and girls had shown up more than once to my not-so-humble abode.

There were five bodies moving slowly down the hall.

Reaching out farther, I found they had used some type of cutter on the main door. The crashing sound must have been the piece they'd cut falling into the house. I'd no doubt it *wasn't* the intention to have made any noise upon entry, unless they were idiots.

Well, their screwup was our salvation.

"We've got five people incoming," I whispered. "Did you close the bathroom door?"

"Yes," Rachel replied.

"Good." Then, I focused my attention on The Admiral and said, *"You may want to go down now."*

"Can't, man. I'm ready for action."

"We're about to be attacked," I explained. *"Having you standing up isn't going to make fighting all that easy."*

"I'll do my best, pal," he replied, as if shrugging, *"but once I'm ready, I'm ready."*

"Do you want me to slap him or something?" Rachel asked, her face serious as she prepared to fight whoever was coming after us.

"Yes, please," cooed The Admiral.

I grimaced and gave Rachel a look. "I think that would make things worse."

"Right."

I carefully stepped out of the shower as the five bodies moved into place just outside the bathroom.

One last scan allowed me to pinpoint what Rachel and I were dealing with, and it wasn't thrilling.

"Werewolves," I whispered.

The shower was still running so as not to tip off the intruders that we knew they were here. Rachel stayed in, but the showerhead was farther back, meaning she was no longer getting wet.

I handed her the robe she'd dropped and went to reach for a robe of my own, but it was too late.

The handle was turning.

CHAPTER 2

The door swung inward and there I stood, in all my glory, as the first werewolf stepped inside. She looked at my naked body, fixating finally on The Admiral.

She blinked.

I kicked.

The Admiral flopped about.

"Take it easy, pal!" he yelped.

"Shut up."

The werewolf hit the floor, but another dived in behind her and reached out for me. Then, he paused, looking unsure about the prospect of wrestling with a naked guy who had a boner.

A left cross rung his bell, dropping him to the floor with a thump.

Normally it would have taken a few punches to exact this amount of destruction to something as tough as a werewolf, but they were in my house, I was naked, my girlfriend was right here with me, and my adrenaline was through the roof. Plus, again, I had all those enhanced powers from that damn vampire bite.

In other words, it was *not* the best time to fuck with me.

I glanced down at The Admiral at that thought.

Okay, so I suppose it *was* the best time to fuck with me in a literal sense, but you know what I'm saying.

The third werewolf had jumped into the bathroom and he didn't seem to care about my situation. His eyes were red and he had drool pouring from his mouth. He was ready to bite.

The Admiral must have realized that he was not exactly safe in this equation, because he began to deflate.

"*It's about time,*" I said just as the latest wolf dived at me.

I jumped to the side and let him crash into the wall as the remaining two wolves came into the bathroom.

Okay, now it was pretty cramped in here.

"Stay!" I called out as if telling a poodle not to come any closer.

Funny thing was, they did.

For a second, anyway.

Then they looked even more pissed than they had before.

"*Rachel,*" I called to her directly, using our PPD-issued, brain-altering, built-in connection system, "*I'm going to get them out of the way. You head for the door. I'll follow.*"

She nodded.

"Anyone want a treat?" I asked as I kicked back and landed a solid heel against the red-eyed wolf's chest, driving him back toward the wall.

The other two didn't play the game of one-at-a-time fighting. They launched at me with their teeth at the ready.

Unfortunately for them, that was exactly what I was hoping they'd do.

I didn't need to fend off both of them. I just had to knock the one into the other so they'd both be off balance.

My duck-and-punch was perfectly timed.

They both collided with the red-eyed wolf and I took off for the door, right behind Rachel.

Unfortunately, I slipped.

That was one of the fun parts about running around on a wet floor.

I landed right on my ass, too.

My tailbone throbbed in response.

Not fun.

My body healed super fast, which was great, but it was still going to take a minute or so before I would be in tiptop shape. I had a feeling the wolves weren't going to give me a reprieve, though.

"Get the girl," growled the red-eyed wolf. "We'll kill this one."

Well, obviously, I couldn't have that.

And, so, in Bruce Lee fashion, I put my hands behind my head, placing them on the floor, and then I kicked my feet up, hopping straight into the air.

I spun around, wincing at the pain in my back.

"Who the fuck are you guys?" I asked as they paused their advance. "Did I put one of your bosses in the kennel or something?"

Their eyes grew dark.

"Sorry," I said, holding up my hands. "I meant in prison."

"You are our target," said the one I was just going to call Red from now on. "We were paid to kill you and your girlfriend, so that's what we're doing."

"Ah, I see," I said, reaching back to lock the bathroom door. I knew Rachel was going to try and come back in here and I couldn't allow that. Then I stepped forward, careful not to trip over the two unconscious wolves at my feet. "I'm hoping you've realized by now that I'm not easy to kill."

"You'll die before we leave," Red said with a shrug.

"And how many of you will die with me, Red?"

He tilted his head in that way dogs do when they hear a funny sound.

"Who is Red?"

"Oh, uh…" I coughed. "I was just calling you that because you have red eyes. It's not like we've been properly introduced." I raised an eyebrow at him. "If you'd like to give me your actual name, I'd be happy to—"

"Red is fine," he snarled. "It's not like you'll be living long enough for it to matter anyway."

"Right."

I took a mental inventory of where everything was in the room.

There was a razor, but it was one of those electric kinds, so that wouldn't exactly be useful. I suppose I *could* offer each of them a nice clip and a flea dip, but something told me that wasn't a great idea. My hairdryer had potential as a weapon, but I'd have to be quick if I decided to go with that. There were bottles and other stuff *in* the shower, but nothing out here in the open.

Basically, I had my hands and feet, and possibly that hairdryer. Okay, I also had access to magic and fangs and such, but I didn't like using those. They made me feel dirty. I'd always prided myself on my ability with a gun, my hand-to-hand combat skills, and my cunning.

One of the wolves by my feet was starting to rouse, but a swift kick to the jaw put him out again. Just in case, I snapped an extra kick at the second one, too.

Each of those strikes seemed to irk Red, and even his two lackeys were snarling at me now.

"Before you kill me," I said, "would it be okay if I put on a robe first? I mean, I don't really feel comfortable grappling with you guys while my dick is flopping about, and I'd rather not be found lying in my bathroom naked when the police arrive, you know?"

Red rubbed his chin.

"Yeah, okay," he said, holding back his comrades. "But make it quick. We have a few more visits to make tonight before we get paid."

I reached for my robe and began putting it on.

"Anyone I know?" I asked.

"Yeah," he replied with a snarl. "Your other officers."

"Only if we get there first, boss," noted one of his lackeys.

"Quiet!"

I looked up, showing them what smoldering eyes looked like on a fully decked-out amalgamite.

They shuddered in response.

"Yeah," I commented through gritted teeth as I tied a knot on the belt that held my robe together, "I don't think you killing my team is going to work for me."

CHAPTER 3

I knew they were all planning to attack me at once, so I'd have to make the first move if there was any chance of getting through this without suffering too much damage.

Why did I always have to do things the hard way?

"*Open the fucking door, Ian,*" Rachel said through the connector as the handle moved back and forth.

"*Nope.*"

"*I'll blow the damn thing in if you don't,*" she replied.

"*Please don't,*" I said as I saw the muscles rippling on the wolves before me. "*It'll destroy my resale value.*"

"*Then you'd better get over yourself and use magic so you can get the hell out of there.*"

"*I don't like using magic, Rachel,*" I replied. "*You know that. Now, just give me a second so I can get everything under control in here.*"

It was a command, which I knew Rachel was fond of these days. My dark attitude had turned her somewhat submissive as of late. Not really a whips-and-chains type of submissive, but she *did* seem to get off on being bossed around some. It was odd for me since it used to be the other way around.

The Admiral took my thoughts as a cue to start rising up again.

"*Stop!*" I told him.

Fortunately, he listened this time.

Then, with lightning-fast speed, I reached out and snagged the hairdryer from its place on the wall.

Like a ninja flinging a throwing star, I launched the appliance directly at Red.

It was perfectly on target, flying straight toward his forehead.

I thought for certain this was going to be like one of those awesome moves you see in action films.

And it was…until the cord reached its maximum distance, anyway.

It paused for a millisecond in mid-air before flying back at me.

"*What the fuck, dude?*" shrieked The Admiral as the hairdryer collided with him and his downstairs neighbors.

I grunted and crumbled to the ground.

Red began laughing uncontrollably. His goons joined in on the merriment. I'd sufficed in racking myself, which the wolves clearly found hilarious.

"What a moron," Red howled through bouts of laughter. "We should just stand over here and let this dickhead kill himself!"

The others laughed even louder at that.

"What happened, Ian?" Rachel yelled through the connector.

"Nothing," I whimpered.

"Are you okay?"

"I'm fine."

"You don't sound fine."

It took a fair bit of effort, but I stood back up and wobbled on my feet for a moment. Okay, so I wasn't exactly fine. It's amazing how getting knocked in the marbles can take you from being a powerful force of mayhem to a groveling mass of sadness.

"Take your time, dude," Red said, wiping the tears from his eyes. "We can wait to kill you. Besides, maybe you'll accidentally shove your toothbrush up your own ass next or something!"

I frowned at him, thinking that maybe it *would* be a good idea to use magic on him and his stupid cohorts. A nice energy spell would turn their laughs into screams, after all.

It *was* tempting.

Again, though, I wouldn't go there unless I had absolutely no other choice.

If the situation were truly bad enough for me to fear for my life, I'd go with magic in a heartbeat. It wasn't.

Yeah, the hairdryer thing was an oopsie.

Shit happens.

But I honestly wasn't worried about these idiots killing me. I *was* concerned Rachel may be hurt by them, but not me. Of course, if they knocked me out, I wouldn't be able to help her in any way.

I was going to need to make a move.

"Okay, assholes," I spat while faking the need to reach out for the door handle to keep myself steady, "which one of you wants to die first?"

"*Me,*" groaned The Admiral.

"*Dude, shut the fuck up!*"

Red's laughter slowed, but his face was still lit up.

"Oooh," he said, stringing on his crew, "we're so scared."

I smiled at him.

"I love overconfidence," I remarked. "It makes it so damn easy to beat people at their own game."

Red obviously caught on to the fact that something was suddenly amiss because he stopped laughing completely. He then growled at his goons until they stopped laughing as well.

"What are you talking about?" he asked.

"Just that you're all idiots," I replied, opening the door and slamming it behind me.

It hadn't given us much time, especially since the door locked from the inside, but it allowed me to grab Boomy from his holster while Rachel got her hands glowing.

Boomy, my Desert Eagle .50 caliber gun, glistened under the overhead lights. I loved him like a son. It was because he was such a badass that I'd had to name him.

Before you ask, *yes*, I sometimes talked to Boomy.

And, *no*, he did not talk back.

The door latch to the bathroom turned and three wolves fought to get out at the same time.

"Me first, idiots," yelled Red as he stepped out to meet his demise.

Boomy was not forgiving.

When a breaker bullet left my gun, it did so with vicious intentions. Breaker bullets were the projectile of choice for the Vegas PPD because they contained shards of wood and silver, and they also housed negation strands. When the bullet struck someone, these items launched throughout the body explosively. The wood would inevitably strike the heart of a vampire, killing them; the silver would fly through a werewolf and take them out; and the negation strands worked swell against magic users. You didn't really need anything special to kill a pixie because the .50 caliber bullet would completely annihilate one of those little bastards.

Some officers had started adopting a new type of projectile that was growing in popularity among Retrievers. Those were the cops from the Netherworld who came topside to bring back supers who had outstayed their welcome. They'd been using Death Nails, which were similar to breakers, but they looked more like, well, nails. One nice thing about those was that you could drive them into a person by hand. You didn't have to fire them. But they were yet to be approved for use by non-Retrievers.

Fortunately, Rachel held her magic in check, obviously noting that my breakers had done a fine job of eradicating Red and his two goons. I really didn't want fireballs and ice storms flying through my condo.

"What about the two you knocked out?" she asked. "Are they still alive?"

I nodded at her.

"Cuff them and put in a call to Lydia to have Portman send a crew out to pick everyone up," I said as I rummaged through Red's pockets. There was nothing. Not even a cell phone. Finally, in his hip pocket, I found a set of car keys. "We've got keys. The remote will help us find the car. Hopefully there'll be something in there we can use."

"Good," replied Rachel. "Lydia said Portman will have some folks on the way. I told her the door was open and that we'd probably be gone before they got here."

"Yep," I agreed. Then I gave her a kiss. "We'll have to finish what we started in the shower later, okay?"

She gave me a disturbed look. "Well, it's not like I'm interested in doing it now."

"*Me either*," agreed The Admiral in a sullen voice.

CHAPTER 4

According to Red's key fob, his car was a Mercedes of some sort, but I didn't know what model. I pressed the 'panic' button, hoping to hear the horn blare on his car.

Nothing.

"Maybe his car is in the garage," Rachel said, leading the way.

We walked around, hitting the button, but nothing sounded. Finally we headed outside and crossed the street toward Tommy Rocker's, thinking maybe the goons parked that way.

Still nothing.

"Maybe it's dead," I stated, looking at the fob.

"Or he disabled it somehow," suggested Rachel. "Either way, that's not going to do us any good."

"Guess not, which really…" I paused as I glanced up and saw a beat-up white '76 Impala. I flipped over the fob and spotted a white 'i' painted on it. Yes, it was even in lowercase. "Huh," I sniffed, showing the fob to Rachel.

"What kind of idiot carries around an electronic key fob for a Mercedes when they drive a junker like that?"

I was thinking the same thing. Clearly it couldn't be used to open the car door, unless he'd gotten someone from Mercedes to install an alarm for him. I highly doubted they'd comply with such a request.

No, something else was going on.

"Maybe it's his wife's?"

Rachel gave me a look. "So he drives a piece of shit like this and she gets a Mercedes?"

"Could be that he's divorced."

"I suppose that's true," she admitted with a half nod while staring at the car. "Poor bastard."

"Yeah," I scoffed, remembering his intention to kill us both. "Well, he's in a better place now."

Rachel chuckled and followed me to the car.

I didn't believe it would actually be locked, but it was. What could he possibly have in this old wreck that anyone would want?

After cracking open the doors, we started going through the car, piece by piece. There was nothing in the front or back, so we opened the trunk, fully expecting to see a body in there.

We weren't disappointed.

There was most certainly a body in there, but it was alive, and it looked pretty pissed off.

"Turbo?" I said, staring down at the little pixie who worked as the lead tech for the PPD. He was wearing his standard police officer's uniform and everything. "What the hell are you doing here?"

"Those fucking dildo fondlers locked me up in here!" he blurted. Then he growled to himself while making fists with both hands. "If I get my hands on those rump rangers, I'll sign them up for the Butt Plug of the Month Club!"

While it was absolutely normal for pixies to swear like sailors and to come up with creative names to call people, it was totally out of character for Turbo. He was more the nerd type of pixie than the cursing type. For him to be spewing out vulgarities meant he was incredibly fired up.

"Did they get you at your house?" asked Rachel.

"Of course they got me at my house, you slutty jizz target," he spat back, but then he slapped a hand over his mouth as his eyes went wide. Finally, he took his hand away and said, "I'm *sooo* sorry I just said that."

Rachel was typically not the type who tolerated being spoken to in such a way. To be fair, she *had* requested that I call her names as of late while we were roleplaying, but that was an anomaly due to our new situation. With other people, though, she was known to leave a shoe in your ass if you treated her with anything less than respect.

Fortunately for Turbo, she understood he was merely flustered and therefore let it go.

"It's all right," she said, reaching out and patting him on his head gently. "I know you didn't mean it."

Both Turbo and I sighed in relief.

"Thanks," he said, lucky to still be in one piece.

"What I don't understand," I said while eyeing the

pixie, "is why Red didn't just kill you? Seems like that would have been his smartest move."

"Who's Red?" asked Turbo as he scratched his head in thought.

"That's the name I'm calling the werewolf who had red eyes."

"Ah, him." Turbo shrugged. "I don't know. I couldn't really hear them while I was stuck in the trunk. There was a lot of mumbles and growls, but nothing I could make out." He then held up a finger. "They grabbed me just after I left my house to head into work. Shoved me in his pocket. Fucking clit thumber." He scowled for a moment. "Anyway, I could hear him from inside that pocket, and he *did* mention something about collateral."

Maybe that meant Red had planned to use Turbo as a bargaining chip to get to me, should the need arise? Or maybe he needed to keep one of us alive so his employer couldn't just up and kill him when the job was done? Honestly, I wasn't sure what the logic was there, but I couldn't think of any other reason to keep Turbo around.

"I don't know," I said, looking down at the keys again. "I don't suppose you have a clue why this guy was carrying around a Mercedes key fob, do you?"

"No," Turbo replied, waving at me to bring it closer to him. "Hmmm...the side is slightly opened." He pulled out a tiny flashlight and looked inside. "There's another key in there."

"For what?"

"How should I know, you gargantuan nipple pimple?" he fumed, and then he softened again. "Dang it! I'm sorry." He breathed out heavily. "I have to relax."

"It's cool, man," I said. "Why don't you come out of there and get some fresh air?"

He pointed at his ankle. There was a little chain attached to it.

"Oh, shit," I said. "I didn't see that before."

"I would have just picked the lock," he said, "but there isn't one. The guy connected it and then magic sealed it in place."

Rachel leaned in and fired off a little spell that broke the device from Turbo's leg, freeing him. He flew out and zipped around the area like a little bird who had just tasted flight for the first time.

"Thanks, Rachel," he said as he flew back and landed on my shoulder. "I really didn't want to spend the rest of my days in the back of a crap car like that."

I turned to my partner.

"Good thing we decided to look through the car," I said via the connector, not wanting Turbo to think about how he might have actually died in there. *"That would have been a nasty way to go."*

"Quite," she agreed.

"Well," I said aloud, "we should probably—"

"Chief," came the voice of Chuck, one of my other officers, *"Griff and I need help pronto. We're being attacked by something...uh...well!"*

"Werewolves?" I asked.

"Nope," he replied. *"Definitely not werewolves."*

"Right. Vampires, then?"

"I am a vampire, Chief," Chuck replied. *"I think I might recognize those without much fuss."*

"Sorry," I said, taking a breath while realizing I was

being an idiot. *"We just got attacked by werewolves who were apparently hired to assassinate us."*

"Hopefully they didn't succeed," Chuck remarked.

"Funny. So what are you dealing with, then?"

"Are you sitting down?" Griff asked before Chuck could reply.

"No."

"Well, you might wish to do so," Griff replied after a moment. *"From what I'm seeing here, I believe we may be dealing with your...brothers."*

I sat down.

CHAPTER 5

*M*y brothers? How would that even be possible? Unless we were all split up when we were kids or something. But wouldn't we have known about each other somehow? Perhaps I wasn't the only one who was given a trust fund from my parents after all. Having a few wealthy dudes who all had similar backgrounds would be too coincidental and would definitely warrant investigation.

I explained the claim to Rachel and Turbo, and then patched them in on the call.

"*Sorry, guys,*" I said as I rubbed my temples, "*did you say you saw my brothers?*"

"*They're not dead ringers for you, Chief,*" Chuck answered, "*but they're casting spells, their fangs are out, and they've got that werewolf eyes thing going.*"

"*And they are also clothed in fine attire,*" Griff added.

So they *were* amalgamites.

Well, damn.

I thought I was the only one.

"Do they look like me at all?"

"Just in that they're attractive and well-dressed," Griff answered.

"How many of them are there?" asked Rachel.

"Two," replied Chuck.

"Chief," Jasmine chimed in a moment later, *"we've got a couple of amalgamites trying to break into my flat here."*

"We've?" I asked, raising an eyebrow at Rachel.

"Felicia, Serena, and Warren...uh...spent the night."

"Nice," said The Admiral.

I ignored him, though I had to agree. Well, subtracting Warren from the equation anyway. I knew that Felicia and Jasmine had played together before, and I was also well aware of Serena's lust for carnal things, but I had no idea they all got busy orgy-style. My guess was that this had to do with them having met the valkyries during our last mission. Those Amazonian babes could start the engine on a rusted-out jalopy.

There was no time to allow my mind to drift into that fantasy at the moment.

I was more worried about the amalgamites stuff.

On the one hand, it'd be great to finally have people in this damn world who understood the things I went through on a daily basis; on the other hand, if they were bad guys—which it seemed they were, that would mean I had a major fight looming in my future.

A little voice in my head told me that something fishy was going on here.

"We can't beat these things off," Chuck said.

I fought not to giggle at that, but Rachel's juvenile grin

made that challenging. Ever since she'd turned to the submissive side, she'd become more in tune with my appreciation for naughty humor.

"Griff's been casting spells at them like it's going out of style," Chuck continued, *"but they just heal each other and resume their attack."*

"Same on this side," said Felicia. *"Jasmine's been hitting both of them repeatedly with fireballs. They just keep coming and coming."*

"Definitely sounds like they could be your brothers," noted Rachel aloud, her smile in full force.

Honestly.

"Okay, guys," I said, *"get out of there and meet me down at the station."*

"There's no getting out, Chief," Warren stated as Rachel, Turbo, and I took off back toward The Martin so we could get to my car. *"They've got runes all around the house. These guys planned this attack really well."*

"We have the same situation," announced Griff. *"It's only a matter of time before they break through my defenses."*

Shit.

All of my officers were trapped, and it appeared they were being hemmed in by beasties who were just like me. If I had to fight my team one on one in my normal mode, I wouldn't have a shot. But if I was decked out like I was now, due to that vampire bite, then I could probably destroy them all without much of a fuss.

That told me that my 'brothers' weren't as powerful as me, though they clearly had multiple facets of their makeup unleashed. Of course, it could also be that they were holding back for some reason. Maybe they weren't actually interested in killing my team, but rather just taking them hostage like Red had done with Turbo. Another option might be that they preferred to kill by hand. They'd use magic and such to get inside, but then they'd finish the deed in some dastardly way.

I hoped the latter wasn't the case, but I wasn't about to risk it.

"*Lydia,*" I called back to the PPD artificial intelligence dispatcher, "*have you been listening in?*"

"*Yes, puddin',*" she replied.

This was a little concerning because she had expressly told me before that she *never* listened in unless she was invited to the call. Now, to be fair, it could have been that she was conferenced in automatically when everyone else joined. Still, with the Directors acting strange over the last number of months, everyone on my crew knew that we had to be careful not to divulge too much information when it came to things like this.

"*Great,*" I said, playing as if it didn't bother me in the least. "*I need you to get emergency transport authorizations to the Netherworld PPD for the entire team.*"

"*I'll work on it now, honey cakes,*" she replied.

"*Thanks, babe,*" I said, playing my part in the flirting so that her chips would keep buzzing. "*You're the best.*"

"*I'll bet you say that to all the AI dispatchers.*"

Considering there was only one that I worked with, no. Clearly, Lydia had been reading through tomes of sinful romances again. It was obvious whenever she did this because she'd pick up a subtle line or two to use on me.

"Only you, Lydia," I replied as we got to my Aston Martin. *"Only you."*

Rachel rolled her eyes at me, but she knew the deal. I played the game with Lydia and she gave me special treatment. Her digital crush on me had saved our hides more than once over the years, though, and that meant Rachel didn't gripe too much about my relationship with our dispatcher.

"It appears that the Netherworld PPD has been under attack recently, love muffin," Lydia declared. *"There have been riots in the main city center."*

"Well, that's not good," I replied.

"They won't allow any transports to the main station, but there are satellite locations we are authorized to use." A split-second later, she added, *"I have a better option, though. I've done a check on the team records and it appears that all of you are due for a reintegration cycle within the next forty-five days."*

I squinted and asked, *"How does that help us?"*

"You may attend reintegration any time you wish, as long as you are within a forty-five day window of your due date."

I hadn't known about that. Most supers went out of their way to squeeze every last moment being topside before going through reintegration. That's because the process sucked. It took you out of your usual routine, and it reset your due date accordingly. In other words, why would anyone want to go early when it just meant that their next reintegration clock would be reset to that day?

But we needed to get out of here, so we'd deal with it.

"Fine," I answered for everyone, knowing they'd likely

rather take their chances with the amalgamites instead of face reintegration. *"Hook us all up, please."*

There was a group groan.

"All of your tattoos have been configured," Lydia replied. *"You may leave at any time."*

We didn't use our tattoos very much as topside cops, but the easiest way to transport down for your reintegration cycle was through the ink. You could use a portal station instead, if you wanted, but that seemed like a waste of time to me.

"Perfect," I said. *"Thanks, Lydia. Everyone, activate your transports now."*

I didn't wait for their replies, assuming they knew my words were intended as a command not a suggestion.

"What about us?" Rachel asked as Turbo landed on her shoulder.

My initial reaction was that they should head down to safety as well, leaving me up here to see who my 'brothers' truly were, but I had the feeling that not even I could handle four amalgamites.

If I was to face them, I'd need to truly come to grips with my newfound skills.

That meant training.

I hated training.

Not as much as reintegration, but unfortunately I was going to get to do both.

Yay.

"Activate your tattoos," I said with a sigh. "We have some work to do."

CHAPTER 6

I was glad to see my team had made it safely to the Netherworld, but I didn't think any of us truly wanted to be there.

Me, especially.

I was the one who had to go through all sorts of crap because of my various genetic bits.

The others on my crew only had to deal with their particular race-based issues. Chuck would be put through blood-avoidance training; Felicia would have her hunting instinct tamed; the mages would go through power management courses, which were designed to keep them from attempting to gain dominion over the normals; Turbo would be reminded why he should keep his language to a minimum and also how *not* to fling dust at everything; and Warren would undergo self-assurance entrainment so he wouldn't attempt to summon demons while topside.

For now, though, we were all here and everyone seemed to be in decent health.

"Are any of you injured?" I asked.

"I have a few welts on my bottom," Warren admitted, "but it wasn't bad enough that I needed to invoke my safe word or anything."

I looked at him. "Ew."

"Oh, wait," he said as his face turned red, "you meant because of the attack, didn't you?"

"A little bit, yeah," I replied before studying the rest of my crew. "You're all fine?"

They nodded.

"Good."

"Next in line," called out a burly looking woman who was obviously a werebear. She then pointed at Warren. "Let's go, pal. I haven't got all day."

Warren glanced at us and shrugged as he walked up to get his paperwork underway.

"Any idea who those people were?" asked Chuck. "I thought you were the only amalgamite around?"

"I thought the same thing," I answered, sighing. "I don't suppose any of you took pictures of them?"

There was a collective squint.

"We were somewhat preoccupied with trying to stay alive, I'm afraid," Griff answered for the team.

"Next!"

I motioned for Turbo to go get his paperwork done. He already knew my side of the story anyway.

"The thing I don't understand," I began, "is why they sent amalgamites after all of you, but only sent a team of werewolves to wipe out me and Rachel."

"That does seem odd," mused Griff. "The first thing that comes to mind is that they weren't planning to kill us. Rather, they were just going to capture us to use as a bargaining chip should you somehow survive the assassination attempt."

I nodded slowly, since that was similar to what I'd been thinking. But I couldn't get myself to fully accept that scenario.

"It just doesn't add up," I said finally. "Four amalgamites have a much better chance of killing me than five werewolves."

"Valid point," Griff conceded.

"Next!"

I motioned Rachel to go forward. She gave me a stern look. I gave her a sterner look. Her eyebrows wiggled as a mischievous grin crept upon her face. Then she skipped up toward the line.

Weirdo.

"It could be that whoever sent the wolves only intended *you* to be kept occupied," Serena suggested. "That would give the amalgamites the chance to kill all of us unimpeded."

I didn't like the sound of that, though it was probably the most likely solution to this puzzle.

"That actually sounds reasonable," I said after a moment. "It would make it so you couldn't come and cover my ass once they decided to turn on me, too."

"Exactly," Serena agreed.

Now the big questions were *who* put out the hit on all of us and *why did they do it?* My guess was we had another uber in town. That seemed to be the only time weird shit like this happened. But an uber who could churn out amalgamites seemed rather unlikely, unless he gave them a shot or something that…

I turned to Griff. "Could a mage or wizard infuse the people you saw with something to make them appear to be like me?"

"You mean dapper?" asked Chuck with a smile.

I rolled my eyes at him. "Are you on a comedic kick lately or something?"

"The mage would have to be rather powerful," Griff answered before Chuck could reply. He was looking away thoughtfully. "It wouldn't last for long, either, but I suppose it could be done."

"So an uber like that Reese guy who had the demon batteries?" I ventured. "Someone like him?"

Griff gave me a hesitant nod. "Again, it would take an enormous amount of power."

"Next!"

Felicia headed off toward the clerk.

"All right," I said as she walked away, "the most likely situation here is that we have another uber on the loose. But this one must have seen what happened to the last ubers who attacked the town."

"We destroyed them," Jasmine stated.

"Yep."

"So, instead of attacking the town," added Chuck slowly, "this uber has decided to come after us first."

"Exactly," I said, pointing back and forth between my two officers. "And coming down here has probably put the uber on his heels."

I didn't know if that was true, of course, but it made

sense. Assuming it was a mage running all of this, I'd imagine that he'd first want to make certain the PPD was out of the picture. He'd know that reinforcements would eventually arrive, but by then he could be entrenched.

"It could be a *she*, you know," Jasmine noted in a haughty way. We looked at her. "I'm just saying that you immediately assume it's a guy, but it may be a woman."

I gave her a sidelong glance.

"So it bothers you that we assume someone who is being a monster-sized dick is a dude?"

"Well, when you put it like that…" She trailed off. Then, she sighed. "It's just that women are equally capable of being monster-sized dicks."

"No argument here," I said. "There was a particular dragon not too long ago who wanted to feed us to her children, as you may recall."

"Precisely," Jasmine bragged. "That's what I'm talking about."

"Okay, then," I said, giving in with a shrug. "From now on, we'll consider the brains behind this incredibly assholeish situation to be a chick."

Jasmine held a look of accomplishment on her face, and she even stood a little taller.

"Thank you."
"My pleasure."
"Next!"

CHAPTER 7

I sat at the little table, looking across at the woman who was processing my paperwork. Yes, paperwork. You would think that with all of the technological advancements, they'd be doing everything digitally, but not so with the reintegration offices. Oh, they would transfer everything from paper to the computer at the end of the day, but they wanted to make sure it took as long as possible while you were undergoing the process of reintegration.

Supposedly, this had to do with calming the mind of the person being reintegrated.

Fail.

"Are you still an amalgamite?" she asked, pushing her mousy brown hair from her eyes.

What an odd question. That was like asking someone if they were still human. How could that possibly change?

I should have just said "yes" and moved along, but I couldn't.

"How could I have changed into anything else?"

She blew out a long breath, making it clear that she no more wanted to be asking these questions than I wanted to be answering them. Then, she set down her pen and sat back, crossing her arms. This was the universal signal that it was go-time.

"You are a unique person, Mr. Dex," she replied coolly. From what my crew said about their attackers topside, that may no longer be true. "Therefore," she continued, "we have no precedent regarding what you are or are not capable of doing."

"But that's just dumb," I countered. "Do you ask vampires if they are still vampires?"

"We don't need to," she answered, her voice as tight as mine. "There are thousands of years of data showing that vampires cannot transform into anything other than vampires." She held up a finger. "And don't bring up the point about them turning into bats. That's folklore, and you know it."

"I wasn't going to bring that up," I noted, crossing *my* arms. "I'm not stupid enough to believe that hoopla."

Her plump cheeks were getting redder by the minute. Obviously, she had to deal with difficult people all day, but I was feeling singled out here. As she'd just admitted, she wouldn't have asked that particular question to anyone else, making it prejudicial.

With dull eyes, she pushed forward. "I'm assuming the answer is 'no' to you having changed from being an amalgamite?"

"I have not changed, nor will I ever change." I uncrossed my arms and sat forward as well. "Is there a way that you can put that in there so I'm not asked this silly question the next time I come down here?"

"No," she replied, "and what's the big deal anyway?"

"Seriously?" I scoffed. "How can you even ask me that? It's offensive and racist to question if I've changed from being what I was born to be."

Her look was not one that conveyed sympathy.

"Okay," I added in a huff, "how would *you* like it if someone asked if you had changed from being a werebear?"

She shot me a look.

"I am *not* a werebear!"

That made me do a double-take. She was easily six and a half feet tall, two hundred and fifty pounds, and had more hair on her arms than Harvey and Portman put together.

"Seriously?" I said, furrowing my brow in disbelief.

"I'm a fae, thank you very much."

I blinked.

"You're kidding," I said, looking her over again.

"I have a pituitary issue."

Ouch.

Well, I felt like a rather enormous asshole at that moment. Typically, werebears were *proud* of the fact that they were big and hairy, but for a fae this had to be catastrophic.

"I…uh…well…"

"Again, Mr. Dex," she growled like a werebear, "are you *still* an amalgamite?"

I looked down in shame.

"Yes."

"Super." She uncrossed her arms and started writing again. "Married or single?"

"Single, but I have a girlfriend."

"Don't care," she replied. "Are you still the chief of the Las Vegas Paranormal Police Department?"

"Yes."

"Are you still living at The Martin?"

"Yes."

"Do you still drive a red Aston Martin?"

"Yes," I replied, though I found that a weird question as well.

She went quiet for a few moments as she continued her writing.

I tried to think of a way to apologize for being a douche coconut, but anything I could think to say would just make things worse. Honestly, I felt like I'd just asked an overweight woman when she was due. And, yes, I *had* done that before.

"Please list all of the race types and classifications that are a part of your genome."

"Vampire, werewolf, djinn, wizard, mage, pixie, fae, uh…werebear, weresheep, wererabbit, weretiger—"

She glanced up. "Weretiger?"

"Correct."

The pen went down again and she tilted her head at me.

"You're sure?"

How could I *not* be sure?

"I'm sure," I said without inflection.

"That would make you only one of three surviving weretigers in existence."

"Partial weretiger," I corrected, "and, yes, I'm aware of that fact."

Weretigers had nearly gone extinct during the last major war in the Netherworld. This happened during a combined attack from the werewolves, fae, werebears, and pixies. The tigers hadn't had a chance, meaning only a handful remained. Unfortunately, they never procreated to extend their line.

The remaining tigers were too busy reading books and playing around on social media sites, making it so they never had time to build relationships.

After a while, all but two of them died off.

One female and one male.

The male, a weretiger by the name of Mike, refused to mate with the remaining female, Bethany, because he preferred the company of gentlemen. Worse, he wouldn't donate a sample of his baby batter because that would require him to touch himself, which disgusted him something fierce. The reason for this was because he was one of a very few supernaturals who could have discussions with his penis…much like I did with The Admiral. Well, his penis turned out to be female, and thus he found the prospect of doing anything sexual with her, even on the plane of self-pleasuring, distasteful. I didn't quite understand this being that I'd smack The Admiral about if the need arose. I wasn't gay, but maybe Mike hadn't found a way to shut up his penis the way I had mine.

My first thought was that a nice bite or scratch would infect someone and turn them into a weretiger, and that was true. But unfortunately, the remaining tigers wouldn't play that game for a few reasons. Bethany was extremely timid. If you were to say 'boo!' to her, she'd curl up in a ball and wait for the end to come. Even if she *had* managed to fight back, though, it wouldn't have mattered because she'd had herself declawed many years ago. As for Mike, he had his nails done on a regular basis and he wouldn't dare do anything to mess them up. Besides, the only thing he bit into on a regular basis were pillows. Suffice it to say that those two weren't exactly the proud warriors that weretigers were once known to be.

"If you would be willing to rub one out in a cup," she said seriously, "we could possibly restart the line of weretigers."

Her use of the phrase "rub one out" only made it more challenging to believe she was a fae.

"Rub one out?" I said with a grimace, not asking for clarification but more to point out that the term was not becoming of a lady.

She clearly didn't catch my intended meaning, though, and therefore began listing other terms for the act.

"Yeah," she said. "You know what I'm talking about. Tug your tugboat, slap your salami, yank your crank, fondle the fella, burp the worm, feed the chickens, drain the dragon, hit the ham…" She took a deep breath. "Pull the pickle, play the organ, launch the hand shuttle, rub the unicorn horn, wax the weasel, date your palm, hug the turtle…" She paused and looked up. "That last one has been going around in the Netherworld recently."

"Wonderful," I said, feeling like I'd just bitten into a lemon.

"Let's see, there's also—"

"No, no," I interrupted, waving my hands at her. "I get it."

"So you'll do it?" she asked excitedly. Then she raised an eyebrow at me. "I mean, you could also just fuck her, if she's keen on that."

There was *no way* this woman was a fae.

"No, thank you," I replied, stone-faced. "Look, there's an emergency situation happening topside at the moment and I really need to get through this process in order to return there. So can we please move this along?"

"That depends," she said, staring at me. "Are you going to help the weretigers or not?"

I sighed. "Right."

CHAPTER 8

I almost felt dirty as I sat in the next room waiting for round two. I was sure Rachel would be understanding regarding my agreement to donate to the weretiger cause, but it wasn't exactly a conversation I wanted to have. And I definitely had *zero* desire to give the old handshake to The Admiral.

"Yeah," he said, *"I'm not really fond of that idea either. Maybe Rachel will do it for us?"*

"Not now," I replied.

"Well, no shit, dude. Getting a handy during reintegration is even too weird for me."

"I meant that I don't want to discuss this right now," I clarified. *"I have other things on my mind."*

The rest of my team had already moved along to the next phase before I'd gotten into this room. Of course, they'd all breezed through the paperwork part of the process, so they had a head start.

My biggest worry at the moment wasn't reintegration,

though. It was trying to figure out who the hell these new amalgamites were. It was still baffling to think that they even existed. Try to imagine believing you were the only person left in your family. For all your life, you knew it to be the case. There were no parents, grandparents, siblings, or even cousins. You were completely unique and alone in this world. Then all of a sudden you found out you've got four others who are just like you.

It was trippy.

A worker opened the second processing chamber door on the right. He was wearing a green outfit and white gloves. In his hand was a chart that sat on a standard clipboard.

"Mr. Dex?" he called out, though I was the only person in the room. "Mr. Ian Dex?"

"Yeah," I sighed, getting up and heading over to him. "I'm right here."

"Your tattoo, please?"

I turned over my arm and the guy scanned it. He then verified my name, occupation, date of birth, where I lived, and the car I currently owned.

Finally, he said, "Are you still an amalgamite?"

My head dropped to my chest.

"Yes," I groaned in reply.

He checked a box on his form. "Please enter the chamber, remove all clothing and place it in the plastic bin on the right. Once you've completed that, have a seat on the chair and the computer will provide you with the next steps."

"All right."

He stepped out and I took off all my stuff, carefully

folding it so I could tell if anyone messed with it while I was in the *mind fuck* machine. Yes, that's what I called the damn thing.

Finally, I looked at the chair and let out a long breath.

The entire process of reintegration sucked, but the chair was the worst part. It was covered with fresh plastic for each person who sat on it...I *hoped* it was fresh, anyway. That plastic stuck to your skin and it was cold, but knowing what could happen during this step in the process, I completely understood why they employed its use.

On top of the chair was what looked like a hairdryer, and not the kind that smacked me in the nuts earlier, either. I'm talking about those types you see at the hair salon hanging over people's heads. But this one was different in that it covered your eyes and everything. Okay, so maybe a motorcycle helmet was a better description. Regardless, the thing was clear and it had wires running from it to the ceiling.

That's where the fun was housed.

I took a seat, adjusting myself until the plastic was as comfortable as could be expected. Then I put my hands on the arm rests and waited.

Straps came out and locked my arms and legs in place as the helmet lowered onto my head. This was not a place you wanted to be if you were claustrophobic, let me tell ya.

Once the helmet was on, it turned from clear to pitch-black.

I couldn't see or hear a thing.

"Mr. Dex," said a computerized voice that was just

above a whisper, "you are about to undergo the entrainment phase of reintegration."

Here is where all the magic happened. It would feel like you weren't being altered or anything, but something happened in this unit that caused your beliefs and base desires to get tinkered around. I didn't understand how it worked, and I didn't really care. I just wanted it to be over with so I could get back to the real world.

The computer continued.

"You will feel renewed and refreshed at the end of this cycle." That was bullshit. "Everything that happens during this level of reintegration will be deemed confidential. Please note that you may become slightly disoriented. This is normal. However, if you find yourself agitated or wracked with a sudden desire to soil yourself, please let us know." It was said with such a sweet voice, too. "We hope you enjoy your entrainment procedure."

And that's when the music started.

CHAPTER 9

The music was classical, but there was a warbling sound that I could hear playing underneath it.

Based on the literature I was forced to read when I'd joined the PPD, the warbling happened at a particular frequency that synced with your brain. After a certain amount of time, the speed of the warble lowered, bringing your brain along with it. Supposedly, this made it so you would slowly fall into a meditative state.

It sounded dubious to me, but I'd be damned if I had ever remembered the last few minutes of the entrainment process.

In conjunction with the sounds, there was a light show. Blues, yellows, reds, and greens bounced around across my visual field. There was no flashing but rather just movement of light.

It was soothing.

Like the sounds, this was supposed to work to calm

the mind, making it receptive to the suggestions that were to follow.

"*Normals are your friends,*" I heard the first whispering words. "*You would never wish to harm a normal.*"

Obviously, this thing hadn't met a lot of normals.

I had to keep thoughts like that away, though. There was nothing in the literature about the entrainment system being able to read your thoughts, but I wasn't going to risk it. I just wanted this to be over with so I could get back to saving my beloved city of Vegas.

Again, I really didn't expect there to be an attack against the people there, seeing as I believed the mage in charge of this little assassination play would want to be certain that we were all dead first. But I wasn't one hundred percent certain of that, either. For all I knew, there were four amalgamites ripping through the Strip as I sat here getting reprogrammed.

"*You would not wish to bite a normal,*" whispered the machine. "*They taste sour and they carry disease.*"

I could feel myself getting groggy already. I hated that, especially because it was out of my control.

It was like getting drunk. You start out thinking you'd just have a couple of drinks, but then your judgment becomes suspect and you end up facedown in the gutter, singing show tunes while some homeless guy steals your wallet.

Not that such a thing had ever happened to me, of course.

Anyway, the whispers now felt like someone was tickling my ears.

"You would find it disgusting to mark a tree in your neighborhood."

At least the computer had moved on from focusing on the vampire part of my psyche to targeting the werewolf part, instead. That was progress anyway. It didn't matter. I knew it would go back through them all over and over again during the next half hour.

"You should always clean up after yourself when you are in the park."

My eyes were already closed, but they were threatening to roll up into my head now.

Just once, I wanted to make it through this entire ordeal fully conscious. I'd always wondered how it wrapped everything up at the end. What was it that it did to make people get violently ill, and why did it always happen to me? Maybe it happened to everyone?

"You are very handsome," said the computer, *"but you should strive to see the beauty in others as well."*

Fae.

I fell asleep for awhile, which I only knew because I jolted back awake and heard the computer say, *"You may feel it's important to call someone creative names, but remember that not everyone appreciates your use of vulgarity."*

So we'd moved on to the pixies.

That was…

I woke up again.

"Your wool is wonderful and has many uses that can benefit not only supernaturals, but normals as well."

I found myself nodding. It was true. I *could* turn into a weresheep and make enough wool to…

The next time I awoke, it was to the sound of faster music. Light was coming back into the world, and there was a smell that indicated something disturbing had occurred.

"It is perfectly normal that you have soiled yourself," the computer said in a relaxed voice. "The plastic will be changed before another person enters the chamber, and you may find cleaning resources directly ahead and to the left. Please be sure to bring your bin of clothing with you."

Feeling like I'd just woken up from an all-night bender, I groaned as I looked down at what I'd done to that poor chair.

"Well, that's embarrassing," I said as I pushed myself up, cringing as the plastic pulled against my skin. "Where's the fucking shower again?"

"Ahead and to your left."

"Right, thanks."

CHAPTER 10

*B*y the time I was showered and off to the next station, my brain had come back to full awareness. Cold showers did that to you. Why they didn't offer hot water, I couldn't say, but it certainly added insult to injury.

"How do you think I feel?" grumbled The Admiral. *"I'm the one who shrinks in cold water."*

I rolled my eyes and walked to the next station. This was the room of odd questions. That wasn't what its technical name was, but that's how I remembered it.

A stool sat in the middle of the room with a light shining directly down on it. Everything else was dark.

I took a seat.

A voice came across the speaker system. "Are you ready to begin?"

It wasn't a computer, but I couldn't see a face or anything. My guess was that the voice belonged to a magic-user since we didn't have any empaths in the supernatural world. Or, if we did, they weren't made public.

Regardless, this person wasn't there to read my thoughts. They were there to *dismantle* my thoughts and activate deeper programming. Any time a person was allowed to go topside, they were programmed with certain triggers that kept them from doing bad things. Many people had learned ways to bypass those triggers over the years, but for the most part, they worked just fine.

"I'm ready," I answered.

I tried to look through the dark to see if someone was actually in the room with me. I had excellent vision in dark situations, but the overhead light made it difficult to spot anyone. My guess was they were behind a one-way glass of some sort.

"Does the worm in the moon sense the water of direct sunlight?" she asked.

I blinked.

"What?"

"How many eggs are there in a field of daisies?"

"Uh…"

"If you were to administer a firm handshake to a square meter of dark matter, would the color green still manifest itself to the eye of a mountain range?"

"Are you smoking weed back there or something?" I asked, though I had to admit that my brain felt like it was tingling. "Wait…maybe you're feeding some funny-weed smoke in here instead?"

"What is one plus seven multiplied by potato?"

"Thirty-six?" I attempted, though I don't have any idea why. It *did* sound right, though. "Yeah, thirty-six."

"Who wrote the woodgrain of endlessness?"

"Your mom?"

Okay, that was probably *not* the correct answer, but it was the first thing that came to mind.

There was clearly something strange going on in this room. The questions being asked were nonsensical, but they were unlocking areas of my mind that felt like gaskets releasing. I couldn't really sense any differences in my thought patterns, aside from being somewhat discombobulated, but I *knew* something was going on that was flipping my head around. By way of example, I never used words like 'discombobulated.'

"Trouble comes in two forms," she said, "but it is never discussed where the edge of volcanic activity starts and the mouse begins. Do you know why?"

That made me feel queazy.

"I'm not going to shit myself again, am I?" I asked.

"It's been said that the whirlwind is naught but the ending of a sentient thought whereby subatomic particles interface with a cereal box. Is this true?"

"I haven't a fucking clue, lady."

The questions went on and on, each seemingly more baffling than the last. The *me* in my head was *not* the *me* I was used to having live in there. Okay, even *I* couldn't understand what I'd just thought.

And that was the problem.

It was like my brain was being scrambled with all these weird questions. In fact, it had gotten so bad that I wasn't even able to answer them any longer. I just sat there drooling as I leaned over and waited for it all to end.

Suddenly, she asked a reasonable question. "What is your favorite color?"

"Huh?" I said, wiping the drool from my mouth. "What?"

"What is your favorite color?" she repeated.

"Teal," I answered, after a few moments.

"Who is your favorite person to have sexual relations with?"

"Your mom," I said again.

It seemed like a more fitting response to that question than to the one about the endless woodgrain thing.

There was a pause, and then she repeated the question. "Who is your favorite person to have sexual relationships with?"

I took a deep breath, feeling much better now.

"Rachel," I answered, "but why does that matter?"

"Is there gold at the end of the rainbow?"

Clearly, I was not going to get an answer to my question.

"No."

"Is there gold *in* the rainbow?"

"Yes."

"Why?"

"Because gold is a color," I answered, returning fully to my normal self as my mind felt sharp and clear. "Are we done?"

"Have you completed your officer evaluations?"

I squinted. "Huh?"

She was clearly the most patient person in the world.

"Have you completed your officer evaluations?"

"Oh, uh…not yet." I pulled my collar. "I still have to do that."

"Why haven't you completed your officer evaluations?" she asked.

"There just hasn't been much time," I answered.

I suddenly felt like I'd rather be getting questions about what it would take for a lightbulb to fuck a tissue box so they could give birth to a sunspot.

"I know I have to get to it," I said finally. "I'll…uh… make it a priority or something."

"Do so," she stated matter-of-factly. "The final phase of your reintegration is complete. Please exit through the door straight ahead and sign the paperwork."

I stood up and walked over to the door. After one last look back into the room, I shrugged and walked out.

CHAPTER 11

The exit paperwork was usually simpler than the entry paperwork, but there were still a number of things to sign and pledges to make, etc.

It was frustrating because I needed to check on things topside.

Unfortunately, it required special authorization to make a connector call from the reintegration chamber. Fortunately, Griff was just exiting the completion area and I called out to him.

"Griff, please see if you can get an authorized call up to Lydia to check on things."

He nodded and walked out.

I knew we needed to get my training going before I could successfully battle the amalgamites, but if they were hitting the town already, I'd have to take my chances in order to stop them.

With a sigh, I plopped down in the chair in front of a kind-looking older gentleman. If I had to make a guess, which I wouldn't do aloud due to the debacle that happened with the werebear/fae from before, I would say he was a vampire. Usually, I could tell straightaway what a particular super was, but sometimes I failed at it horribly. The odd part about thinking this guy was a vampire was him looking like a decent sort. Vampires were known to be rather snooty. Then again, Chuck was a vampire and he was one of the coolest people around.

"Mr. Dex, yes?" the fellow asked.

"Yes."

"Amalgamite, correct?"

"Yes."

"Any changes since your last reintegration?" he asked.

"Yes," I answered without control.

I really didn't want to answer the question at all, but one of the things that happened during reintegration was the unleashing of previous mental programming. That included the need to speak truthfully when asked questions by the officers down here.

He took out a fresh piece of paper. "And they are?"

"I can cast magic like a full mage now," I said, struggling to keep my mouth shut. "I can pop out my fangs, utilize the power of tattoos, hunt like a werewolf, fight like a werebear, curse like a pixie—"

The man held up a hand and tapped the pen on the table.

"As an amalgamite, could you not do all these things before?"

"Not really, no," I answered. "I mean, I could cast spells, sure, but not like I can now. I've always been faster and stronger than most, of course. But the teeth thing? No."

He leaned back. "Is it a problem for you?"

"It makes me lisp something fierce, but Rachel finds it sexy." I paused. "The teeth, not the lisping."

"Rachel?"

"My girlfriend."

"Normal or super?" he asked, his eyes thinning.

"Super," I answered. "She just went through reintegration before I did."

He thumbed through his papers for a moment, picked one out of the bunch, and started scanning it from top to bottom.

"Rachel Cress?"

"Yes."

He jotted something down on her paper before tucking it back in with the rest.

"Are you having any issues controlling these newfound powers, Mr. Dex?"

That was a good question. I wasn't experienced with things yet, but I could control whether or not they fired off. Still, I had the feeling that wasn't what he was asking.

I'd have to word my response carefully, making it truthful but guarded.

"My powers don't happen without my expressed desire that they do," I answered.

He held my stare for a few extra moments before nodding at me. Then he started writing a bunch of stuff out. I wanted to peek down and see exactly what he was putting on that page, but I didn't want to chance getting caught.

"Okay," he said finally. "Is there anything else you'd like to declare before exiting the area?"

"Not that I can think of, no," I answered truthfully.

He picked up a clipboard that had a small stack of papers attached to it. This was the signing phase. Talk about hand cramps. You had to either sign or initial a good fifty times before you were let go.

"Each page will have a red or blue checkmark next to a line," he said, pointing at an example. "The red checkmark signifies that you are to sign your full name, the blue one means you are to initial that spot."

My first few signings were crisp and clean, but after that it started to look like I'd graduated from medical school.

After about fifteen minutes, I finished up and handed the clipboard back to him.

He ran through all the pages, then stamped the front, added his signature, and placed the entire thing in a white tray that sat next to him.

"The only thing remaining is for you to recite the Topside Allegiance, Mr. Dex," he announced. "Please raise your right hand and turn toward the camera."

I did.

"Directly under the camera, you will see the latest Topside Allegiance. I have included your name in the top section." He pointed. "Please read the entire allegiance while keeping your hand firmly in the air."

I cleared my throat.

"I, Ian Dex, solemnly swear to uphold and defend the Topside Allegiance, taking every precaution to avoid causing injury to any normal regardless of any risks that it may cause me or any other supernatural. I recognize that I am being given the liberty to travel topside, but such liberty may be revoked at any time, without cause or provocation." I took a breath. "Furthermore, I understand that I represent the supernatural community as a whole. Therefore, I will do my best to protect normals from other supernaturals as a matter of course." The page scrolled some more. "Failure to keep my promise to uphold and defend the Topside Allegiance may result in my immediate removal from topside, and I may be subject to disciplinary action, which may or may not include deep reintegration, as well as time in prison."

The light dimmed and the text faded away.

"Thank you, Mr. Dex," the man said with a warm smile. "You have satisfied the Reintegration Process Committee requirements and, due to the fact that you are an officer of the Paranormal Police Department, you are not due for another reintegration cycle until this time next year."

"Cool," I said, standing up. "Thanks."

"Please exit through the red door and have a nice day."

He didn't have to tell me twice.

CHAPTER 12

The rest of my crew looked about as shellshocked as I felt. There was something about having your brain scrambled around that made you wonder how much control you truly had over your thoughts and actions.

"Everyone okay?" I asked as I took a seat next to Rachel.

They all nodded, but it looked like nothing more than a reaction to the question and not a conscious answer.

We were out in the hallway that everyone exited to when they were done with reintegration. There were chairs and water fountains and such, but it wasn't what I would consider the most secure place to speak about things. Still, I needed to know what was going on topside.

"Griff," I said, turning toward him, "were you able to get through to Lydia?"

"I was," he replied. "She said everything has been quiet. There have been no reports of foul play from any of the casinos, nor have any of our normal informants called in any complaints."

"Good," I sighed. "That will make things easier."

"What things?" asked Rachel.

"I'm going to need you all to train me to…" I paused and looked around. "Actually, what say we take a walk to the cafe? I'm starving."

They looked at me curiously, but clearly caught on to my concerns about our being watched.

Griff stood up. "I dare say that I'm rather famished myself."

We walked down the corridor and entered the cafeteria. It was mostly empty, which was perfect for us. But we still had to be careful, just in case there were eyes tracking us. The truth was that we were likely just being paranoid. That was a temporary side effect of going through reintegration. Arguably, it was a valid side effect seeing how they played around with your deepest thoughts and beliefs while you were in those chambers. This was all done by choice, though. *We* were the ones who wanted to live topside, after all.

I ordered a couple of fish tacos and grabbed a seat near the back.

Everyone else on my squad clearly had bigger appetites than I did at the moment.

Rachel, Jasmine, Serena, and Warren got pancakes and eggs, Chuck had a steak with potatoes and corn, Griff had salmon and vegetables, Felicia had a big bowl of chili, and Turbo had a burrito that was at least two inches taller than he was. Jasmine carried it to the table for him.

"Okay," I said, after finishing a bite, "I'm going to need

all of you to help me to learn how to use my powers to the fullest." They seemed more engrossed with their meals than with my words, but I continued on. "I'm able to control the power well enough, but I don't know how to maximize it. Each of you are masters at your art. I need your mentoring so I can face my 'brothers'."

There was no argument.

Everyone knew this was an odd situation. Having me at my best was the only way we'd have a chance at defeating a bunch of amalgamites. And based on what I was told before, the others were not as powerful as I was currently. They were more powerful than I'd been prior to being bitten by that damn vampire, though, and that was my worry.

What if they grew in strength eventually?

If that happened, it'd take more than just me to combat them. My team would certainly try to help, but they wouldn't last very long. The only way we'd be able to drop a bunch of amalgamites who had the same level of power as me would be by getting a lot of backup from the Directors. Sadly, they weren't being all that helpful as of late.

Bastards.

"The way I see it," I said, "I'll need to be able to control my magic so I don't wear myself out too soon."

"Agreed," said Griff, who was known for playing more of a defensive role during our bouts with the bad guys. "Self-preservation is paramount to any successful battle."

The pixie in me wanted to call him Captain Obvious, but I held that down.

"True," Rachel said between chews, "but you can't win

a fight if you don't punch back." She then turned to me. "What you'll really need is to learn how to block *and* punch, Ian. With your power, you should be able to do both."

"It'll take some practice, though," Jasmine chimed in.

Nobody argued the point.

I turned to Warren as he was dousing his pancakes with enough syrup to cause the average person to drop into a diabetic coma. How he managed to stay so ridiculously thin was a mystery. It wasn't like the man exercised. I suppose some people just had the metabolism of a hummingbird.

"I'll need you to help me with runes, Warren."

"Sounds good, Chief," he said, not even bothering to look up.

"Chuck and Felicia," I said, glancing over at the two of them, "vampire and werewolf stuff."

"It's mostly about control," replied Felicia while working her knife and fork like a samurai.

"Yep," agreed Chuck.

"Serena—" I started.

"Healing," she interrupted. "Yes, you will need to learn that thoroughly if you are to survive against what we saw earlier."

"Great."

The final person in the bunch was Turbo. He wasn't exactly known for his prowess with Pixie Dust, but he could lay out a stream of obscenities with the best of them. The problem there was that he only did that in extreme situations. He prided himself on keeping his nerdiness at the forefront of his personality, not the vulgarities. The last couple of weeks taught me that I had gotten pretty decent at calling people names in creative ways, anyway. Where I needed Turbo's help was with technology.

I didn't say anything to him, though. He had his coat and hat off, lying on the table next to his plate, and all I could see of him was his lower body hanging out one side of that burrito.

"Well," I said, downing the last bite of my second taco, "as soon as you're all ready, we're going to go see my friends in the Badlands."

All eyes flashed at me, realizing that I meant it was time to visit Valerie and the valkyries.

CHAPTER 13

This was the third time I'd visited with the valkyries, and it was the second time for my crew.

We stood in the center of a large arena. Around it were rows of seats that were occupied by some of the most beautiful women in the universe. They were tall, muscular, battle-hardened, and yet simultaneously carried with them a level of femininity that would be the envy at a Hollywood ball.

Valerie, the leader of the troop, was so incredibly attractive that she made fae look pale in comparison. Her battle gear alone was enough to set The Admiral ablaze, and he was always quick to point that out.

Even Rachel had expressed serious interest in our visiting for some playtime, should my desire for that ever arise.

So far, I had declined.

It was one thing to have a fantasy going about such

activities, but there was something entirely different between fantasy and reality.

Been there.

Done that.

Got punched in the coins.

But, much to The Admiral's chagrin, this wasn't the time for sexual deviances. We had to keep our minds on the task at hand.

"*Speaking of hands—*" began The Admiral.

"*Shut up!*" I interrupted before he could finish his sentence. "*I'm working right now.*"

"*So am I!*"

"Ian Dex," Valerie said, stepping over while sharing smiles with the rest of my team, "you have returned to us again. I am pleased."

"I wish it were under less urgent circumstances," I replied. "It turns out that there is a little flock of amalgamites who are trying to kill me and my team." I scratched my head. "Well, they seemed to be trying to kill them, but we honestly don't know exactly what they want, yet. If I was to guess, though, I'd say they want me to join their ranks." I looked up at her. "They're apparently my brothers."

"How many?" she asked.

"Four," I answered. "That we're aware of, anyway. I suppose there could be more."

"Are they all as capable in the sack as you?" she queried with a seductive look.

"Hey," said Rachel, replacing her valkyries-are-sooo-dreamy look with her I'm-going-to-punch-Ian-in-the-coins look while staring at me. "I thought you said you didn't sleep with them?"

Like I said, fantasy and reality are *not* the same thing.

"Relax, little one," Valerie said, putting her hand on Rachel's shoulder. My girlfriend basically melted at that point. "He did not have relations with us, though we wish he had. We only know of his abilities because we watched him *more* than satisfy a dragon."

"Ew," winced Rachel.

"I *told* you about that, Rachel," I growled. "This was before you and I were back together, as you may recall?"

"Yeah, yeah, yeah," she replied. "Sorry."

"Anyway," I said, tearing my smoldering eyes off Rachel, "I don't know how good my brothers are in the sack. I just know that they're trying to kill, or hurt or whatever, everyone on the PPD, except for me…I think. After that, they're bound to try and take over Las Vegas." I blew out a long breath. "The bottom line is that I have to stop them, and in order to do that, I need my team to help train me."

Valerie's eyes lit up at that.

"Training?" she said as the muscles in her arms rippled. "This is for battle?"

"Yes," I replied, feeling suddenly worried. "Why do you seem excited by that?"

"Because, Ian Dex," she cheered, "battle is our first love. It's even more interesting than sexual adventure."

"*Okay,*" said The Admiral, "*now that's where I'm going to have to disagree with the lady.*"

"*Stow it,*" I commanded him. Then, speaking to Valerie

again, I asked, "I don't suppose you'd care to assist in my training, then?"

"Honestly?" she replied with wide eyes. "That would be incredible. The last time we helped train someone was during the Roman era. It was quite exciting, and we are quite possibly responsible for Rome's many successful conquests."

"How do you fathom that to be true?" asked Griff, who was quite the historian, according to him anyway.

"Because our skill with the blade is legendary."

"Yes," Griff said, "I imagine it is. But are you not responsible for selecting who will live and who will die on the field of battle?"

Valerie looked him over. "It is our first charge, of course."

"Then, my lady, if you trained the Roman soldiers, were you not biased toward their living on the field of battle?"

Valerie opened her mouth and closed it a few times. She even pointed at Griff once or twice. Finally her shoulders slumped and she said, "Damn."

"Do not feel abashed," Griff said finally. "It is the way of men to prey upon the kindhearted. They manipulate at every turn. One merely need only look at the historical records to witness the horror that befalls those who trust."

That brought the mood down in the arena.

Blasted historians.

"Right," I said, bringing the topic back to me and my much needed training. "Even though what Griff said is probably true, I'm not interested in manipulating you, Valerie."

"Sounds quite similar to what Aulus Plautius claimed when he asked us to help train his soldiers," she replied.

"That may be," I countered, "but I'm not looking to conquer the world." I touched her hand. "I just want to stop four amalgamites from taking over Las Vegas."

She looked down at my hand and then back up at me. There was a hint of shine to her magnificent eyes, and her face softened.

"We will help you, of course," she said, "but only if you will agree to discuss terms of pleasuring when we are finished."

I glanced at Rachel. She was all smiles. So was the rest of my team.

"Oh, all right."

CHAPTER 14

Recognizing that everyone on the team was so enamored with the valkyries, except for Chuck and Griff, of course, I had to get them to focus on their training. I told them that *this* was going to be the basis for their annual reviews.

That shaped them up.

My first round was with Serena. The reasoning was that any damage I'd take during training would result in my needing to heal myself. Looking at the musclebound ladies who were itching to kick my ass, this seemed the logical path to take.

Yes, I was already a fast healer, but there was a huge difference between five minutes and five seconds. If you don't believe me, ask your spouse.

"The first thing you'll need to do is control your heart rate," Serena explained as we stood in one of the far corners of the arena, away from the rest of the squad. "It's fine to let your blood pump when healing someone else, but when it's your own body undergoing repair, you need to stay calm, cool, and collected."

"That's so the blood doesn't just squirt out of me like a geyser, right?"

"Partly," she confirmed, "but it's more about making sure your mind stays in the game. In fact, you'd be well advised to avoid looking at your wounds while healing them. It's completely unnecessary to see them as you work, and it's likely to break your calm if you do."

That made sense.

Over the years I'd been injured more times than I could count. As long as I had been able to get away from the battle, or end the battle, I would heal all on my own. Now and then I'd end up in the hospital or subject myself to the healing hands of Serena, obviously, but in most cases my body just did its thing without much fuss. That said, I'd learned early on that it wasn't such a grand idea to look at my wounds. It made me queasy.

"Got it," I said, pushing to keep an active pace going for my training. "What's next?"

"You have a leg up on my abilities in that you can combine your normal magic with your healing magic."

"Mmm...I don't get it," I replied, confused.

"I can only channel healing energy," she explained. "This is a form of magic, but not like the kind used by mages and wizards."

I gave her a double-take. "Are you saying you're a cleric?"

"No, Ian," she laughed. "This isn't a video game."

The moment she pointed that out, I wanted to facepalm.

Here I was, a dude made up of a bunch of genetic mishmash, having tons of skills and knowledge of every race and profession in the supernatural community like nobody else in the entire world—with the possible exception of my 'brothers'—and I was jumping into thoughts of *World of Warcraft* and *Everquest*.

"Right," I finally groaned. "Just ignore me."

"Anyway," she continued, "since you can channel the power of your normal magic along with your healing, you should be able to manage almost instant repair."

She then pulled out a knife from her boot. It was long and curved, with a handle made of white stone with skulls engraved on it. *That* thing belonged in a video game.

After taking a deep breath, she slid the knife along her open hand, causing a long cut to form.

Then, she turned away and closed her eyes.

Her lips were moving almost imperceptibly and I had no idea what she was saying, but the cut began to slowly close until it was finally healed completely. The entire process took roughly thirty seconds. It was mesmerizing.

Once she was finished, she glanced back down at her hand, opening and closing it a few times.

"There," she said, looking a little tired. "Now, that took a little time to heal, but it was still much faster than if I'd bandaged it and just let nature take its course."

"Totally," I agreed.

"How long would it take your body to heal from a cut like that?" she asked. "I mean, without intervention."

"Five minutes?" I guessed.

"That's pretty incredible," she admitted with her eyebrows up. "Then again," she added, "I recall our sessions with the whip when we used to…" She shrugged. "Well, you know."

"Right," I said.

Serena and I had spent a couple of years playing with each other before I'd become the chief of the Vegas PPD. Hell, I'd played with damn near all the chicks on the squad back then.

"*Ah, the good old days,*" The Admiral reminisced.

I had to agree with The Admiral that time. Those *were* the days.

"By the time our afternoon together was complete," she recalled, "your welts were all but gone."

"*Just think how quickly we could recover from them now!*"

"*Shut up.*"

Her eyes were still dancing at the memory.

"But now I'm the chief and I'm with Rachel," I pointed out, "so we should probably stay on topic."

Serena shook her head, bringing herself back to reality.

"Sorry," she said, swallowing. "This place really gets me in the mood, I suppose."

"*Me too, sister,*" said The Admiral. "*Me, too.*"

"Right," I said with a cough. "Well, the question I have is how to channel the healing magic effectively? I've done some basic stuff in the past, but I was never very good at it."

"Ah, that's both easy and challenging," she remarked. "It's challenging to get it right the first few times, but then it becomes second nature and you don't even think about it anymore."

Sounded like when I was firing Boomy, or any weapon for that matter. Or bringing pleasure to the ladies.

"That's more me than you, pal," noted The Admiral.

"I don't just use you for that purpose, remember?" I debated.

"You don't?"

With a sigh, I refocused my attention on Serena.

"I'm listening," I said.

"The trick is to imagine a pure blue light flowing through your body," she said. "Think of it like a beautiful body of water that is full of sparkles from the sun bouncing off a group of flawless diamonds."

"I can do that…I think."

She put out her hand and cut it again. Then she held it up to me.

I reached out and touched my fingers to hers as I closed my eyes.

At first, I found it difficult to concentrate because I was trying to picture water running down my arm. But the water concept was only intended to be an analogy. Once I changed my thoughts to light instead, I felt a soothing warmth flowing from my hand to Serena's. She released a small moan, which didn't make it easy to concentrate.

"That's it, baby," whispered The Admiral. *"You know you want it."*

"For fuck's sake," I growled back at him. *"If you don't stop pestering me, I swear I'll stick you in a chastity device for a week!"*

"Shutting up as ordered," he replied, sounding terrified.

I guess having irritated words with my dick caused a

spark of power to flow through me, because Serena yelped and we both opened our eyes.

The wound was completely healed, and it only took about ten seconds.

"What happened?" I asked.

"You used your magic along with the healing spell." She lifted the knife. "Let's try it again."

"Wait," I protested, grabbing her arm before she could cut herself. "Use it on my hand instead. I've got to learn to heal myself, remember?"

She nodded and sliced away like there was nothing to it.

From my side of the equation, though, I'd have to say it hurt like a bitch. But I couldn't let the pain drive my emotions. This was business. I had to focus and get the job done.

I closed my eyes, imagined the blue light, sent a shock of power down my arm, and yelped as the feeling of being cut reversed itself. It actually hurt worse than the original cut. That was strange, but when I opened my eyes, my hand was completely healed.

"Well, I'll be damned," I said, grinning from ear to ear as I studied my hand. "That's fuckin' sweet."

"You're a fast learner," Serena commented as a sinister smile formed on her face. "I remember that about you."

Thankfully, The Admiral said nothing.

CHAPTER 15

*P*ower and speed were the domain of the werewolf, and Felicia married those two elements better than any wolf I'd ever seen. Even when she was only in partial-wolf mode, she was quite formidable.

"There are three ways we can go about this," she said, reminding me of a sensei I'd studied under years ago. "You can stay in your normal form, go halfsies, or completely change over to wolf."

"My guess is that I'll have to be decently versed in all three modes."

Felicia nodded and looked me over carefully. She walked behind me and was touching various points on my body, kind of like a doctor does during a physical. When she was *directly* behind me, I became a little nervous. Fortunately, she kept on moving.

"Have you turned into full wolf yet?" she asked after returning to stand in front of me.

"Yeah," I replied. "Remember when we were fighting against Sylvester? I went full wolf then."

"No, you didn't," she said seriously. "You were more like a burly poodle."

"That's not true," I shot back, affronted by her tone.

"Did your clothes rip?" she questioned.

I thought back to the fight. They hadn't. They'd barely stretched out at all.

"No," I admitted finally.

"When you bit people, did their limbs snap off?"

"No."

She duck-faced, crossed her arms, and deadpanned, "Burly poodle."

"Fine, then," I grunted, rolling my eyes. "I guess I *haven't* gone full wolf."

"It's not much fun," Felicia said, relaxing her attitude. "I only do it when I really need to, and one of the best things I got when getting my PPD enhancements was to completely control that aspect of my life." She blew out a long breath. "Prior to that, it was…" She looked up at me. "Well, let's just say that the timing wasn't always perfect."

"Right."

"One of the problems you're going to face is that your clothes are not magically enhanced." She then looked up at me questioningly. "Correct?"

"They've recently been updated to handle stains," I answered.

"Right, but they're going to rip apart if you go full wolf in them."

Damn it. She was right. Without the magic tailoring, my suit would be destroyed if I shapeshifted. I swear, it seemed like the universe just wanted me to repurchase suit after suit.

First-world problems, I know.

"Do you think going half-wolf would cause that?"

"No," she said, "and it'll be much easier for you to think properly that way, too. You'll still be highly interested in hunting and fighting, but you'll also have your wits about you." She cracked her neck. "Frankly, I'd bet that you'd be a better fighter like that than if you went full."

"Then we'll just—"

"However," she interrupted, "you won't be nearly as strong or fast."

"I figured as much," I replied, "but these suits aren't cheap, you know."

As soon as this was all over, I was going to have the works done on all my clothing. Every available option, no matter the cost. It was either that or spend countless days trying shit on and spending tons of coin on new suits. To be fair, I *did* rather enjoy shopping for outfits, but it just seemed wasteful to have to throw them away every time they got gooey or bloody. And now that ripping was in the mix, too, I couldn't even justify passing them along to one of those charity places.

For now, I would just do the half-wolf thing and be done with it.

That was a problem, though.

If I didn't know how to go full wolf, I sure as hell couldn't go half wolf either, and without proper guidance, I'd probably end up shredding my suit.

"Okay," I grunted, not wanting to do this at all, "how can I make sure I don't end up in full-wolf mode?"

"Simple," Felicia replied. "All you have to do is stop yourself about halfway through the transition."

I had a feeling it wasn't going to be 'simple.'

"And how do I start the transition in the first place?"

"You already know the answer to that," she replied. "If you didn't, you wouldn't have been able to pick up my scent the way you did when we were at New York-New York battling the goblins."

I gulped, feeling embarrassed about that.

"I…uh…"

"You couldn't have controlled it, Ian," she stated before I could say anything that would make an already awkward situation even worse. "Your pheromones were through the roof, which caused mine to respond in kind. If either of us had morphed, the other would have been ravished."

"*I would…*" The Admiral wisely stopped himself before he could finish that sentence. "*Sorry.*"

I looked at Felicia. "Isn't that going to happen right now, if I change here?"

"Quite possibly," she replied. "But I will fight to keep myself under control. I can't stop you from smelling my scent, though, so that's something *you* will have to combat. If you don't, you'll never be able to fight because you'll be too busy wanting to rut."

"Ah, super."

"*Agreed!*"

So take the horniest guy in the world and then give him the ability to pick up the scent of any woman who is even *remotely* interested in sex. Sounds like a match made in hell.

"What if I can't control it?" I asked.

"I'll shoot you," she replied, pulling out her Desert Eagle. "Now, do you remember what happened the last time you started feeling the wolf inside you as it tried to emerge?"

"Rage," I said after a few moments. "The goblins were trying to harm Rachel and I was pissed off about that."

"Good."

"Good?"

"I don't mean that it's good they were trying to hurt Rachel," Felicia chided. "I mean that it's good you remember the level of rage you felt."

"It's not easy to forget."

"Yes, but it's the amount of anger you channel that will determine how far you morph." She stuck her gun back in its holster. "You never morphed beyond those heightened senses you had at New York-New York, which means you *did* have some measure of control. The difference here is that you're going to have to let yourself go a little further into your rage. Once you've made enough of a change, you can then just let your anger simmer."

"Simmer?"

"Yes," she affirmed. "If you let it build too quickly, you'll lose control of it. If you don't let it build quickly enough, it'll never grab hold." She gave me a stern look. "You need to let it build fast at first, so that the morphing can happen. Then you need to edge it back until you have it under control. If you can manage that, you'll be set."

"Okay," I sighed. "I think I've got it."

I didn't, but there was no way to get things rolling without just letting go and taking a shot at it.

So, rage it was.

I started thinking about things that pissed me off. Not just minor things, but rather those items that made me madder than hell.

People cutting me off on the freeway. Tailgaters. Getting to the bottom of a box of cereal and finding out that there wasn't a toy inside. Wanting a cup of Bones Coffee and finding that we were out…again.

There were thousands of things that could probably do the trick, but I had to be careful what I chose since I didn't want the werewolf to surface at an inappropriate time. I imagined myself turning into a wolf because a little old lady picked up the last box of Entenmann's cookies at the grocery store.

Not good.

The item I finally latched onto was the vision of Rachel hanging in the middle of the werewolf arena in London. That image was burned into my mind for all eternity. *She* hadn't seemed all that bothered by it, but it made me seethe to know that she could have been killed all because Rex, the werewolf, wanted to test his mettle against me.

"Got it," I said.

"Good," Felicia replied. "Now, you need to really push that feeling until the change takes hold."

"How will I know if it's working?" I asked.

She looked at me. "You've heard us howl, right?"

"Of course."

"We do that because it hurts like a bitch when we actually start to change."

"Ah."

I closed my eyes and pictured the scene in London.

It was an inaccurate representation. In fact, it wasn't even the same room. I needed it to be worse and more vibrant. Therefore, I imagined Rachel being tied to a rack with blood seeping from various wounds on her body. She was moaning horribly, whimpering in a way that threatened to make me want to kill anyone and everyone who was within range of my fists.

"Okay, okay," Felicia soothed, "slow it down now."

That's when I noticed the pain in my hands, feet, and face. I opened my eyes and found that everything was clearer than normal. Where I would have expected the colors to be dulled, they were quite the opposite. Glancing down at my hands, I saw they were elongated and my nails stuck out like claws.

I sniffed the air and a low growl escaped my throat as the smell of valkyries filled the room.

While Felicia might be able to fight back releasing pheromones, the warrior babes down here had zero desire to keep themselves in control.

My libido was threatening to take over.

"Control, Ian," Felicia said, which caught me off guard since she usually referred to me as 'Chief.' She moved back into my field of vision, bringing my focus again to her. "You have to maintain control. If you slip up even for a single minute, you'll go full wolf and then there's no telling what you'll do."

My head recognized the logic of her words, but my body wanted to continue down the path it was on.

The physical pain was incredible. A howl began to rise up in my throat, but I fought it with all my might. Releasing that howl would result in the complete destruction of my suit, and I couldn't have that.

Too bad I was losing the battle, at least until I began to recall how the various genetic aspects of my person balanced each other out. If I wanted to avoid going full wolf, I didn't need to manage my emotions, I just needed to allow another facet of myself to gain some hold over things.

But which one?

When I considered vampire, I found that I loathed myself. That seemed logical seeing as how vampires and werewolves weren't exactly the best of friends. I'd hate to have to kick my own ass, though. That would be embarrassing.

Pixie was an obvious choice. A cursing werewolf would be a novelty, if nothing else.

Werebear...no. Talk about a killing machine. That'd just be nuts.

I finally landed on fae. It was the only one, aside from weresheep and wererabbit, that would allow me to maintain half wolf without making it any worse. There may be moments of vanity, but I kind of dealt with that on a regular basis anyway.

"Well, that's interesting," Felicia said with a grimace.

"What?" I replied, my voice sounding slightly different than before.

"You're either the best-looking werewolf I've ever

seen..." She then tilted her head again as if appraising me from an entirely different angle. "...or the ugliest fae."

"Nice," I replied, finding that I could feel the power flowing through my veins, but I wasn't contending with the rage anymore. "The lady who checked us in at reintegration was far less attractive than I look at the moment...I hope?"

"You mean the werebear?" Felicia asked.

"She wasn't a werebear," I corrected her. "She was a fae."

"No fucking way."

"Yep," I stated. "Anyway, I think I've got the hang of this now, and I already know how to fight, so I shouldn't need any pointers there."

"I'm sure you'll do fine," Felicia agreed. "If you *do* ever go full wolf, though, just remember that your bite is worse than your bark."

She then grabbed my chin and looked in my eyes.

"Substantially worse."

CHAPTER 16

Next up was Chuck. I was kind of looking forward to this training stint, to be honest. People had always mistaken me for a vampire over the years, and now that I had the teeth to go with the mystique, I thought it'd be great to know how to use them properly.

"Not a lot to say, Chief," Chuck said, shrugging. "The fact is that we really don't do much more than what you already know how to do. We just get quicker, more agile, have razor-sharp claws, and pointy teeth."

It made sense, actually.

Even Felicia couldn't give me much beyond controlling how far I changed over to wolf form. Aside from that, I got stronger, faster, and could bite through a block of wood. Oh, I could also scratch my ear with my back leg, and I could lick myself. That thought sounded great until I remembered that my dick talked to me.

"*Yeah,*" The Admiral agreed, "*I wouldn't want you licking me either, pal.*"

"What about venom?" I asked.

"*Definitely don't want you biting me, dude.*"

"*I was talking to Chuck, idiot,*" I responded. "Obviously, venom is a thing," I continued aloud, "otherwise I wouldn't even be in this mess in the first place."

Chuck carried a look of dread.

"Yeah, sorry about that." He looked at his feet. "That guy should never have poisoned you."

"Well, he did," I stated hotly. I wasn't mad at Chuck, but the memory of Sly the vampire snapping into my neck pissed me off. "Anyway, it's not your fault that it happened, but I want to understand it in case I need to employ it."

His look of dread changed over to shock.

"You really shouldn't even be thinking about that, Chief," he whispered, glancing around to see if anyone else was within earshot. "That can get you into deep reintegration."

"If used against a normal, yes," I countered. "I was talking about the potential of hitting a super with it."

He shook his head. "That's almost as bad. It wouldn't put you in for a deep brain sweep, because you're a cop, but you could still end up in jail, and your topside privileges would be revoked indefinitely."

"I know the law, Chuck," I reminded him, "and I have no intention of using it unless I have no other choice. But I want to know *how* to use it, should the need arise."

Chuck appeared very uncomfortable with this entire topic. I got that. If he gave me the insider scoop on how to inject venom and rule over someone, he'd essentially be an accomplice…at least to his way of thinking. The truth was that *all* vampires were taught this basic element of their race, except for those who thought the practice should be banned forever, of course. Regardless, Chuck clearly knew how to do it himself, which meant someone imparted their knowledge to him.

"You were trained in this, right?" I asked, knowing his answer.

"Yes."

"And you gained that knowledge when you were just a kid, true?"

"I was twenty-one."

"Which is essentially a toddler in vampire years," I pointed out. "I'm older than that, I'm *slightly* more mature than a twenty-one year old, and I'll get someone else to teach me if you refuse."

He shot me a look.

"Sorry, man," I said with a shrug, "but if I'm going to be facing down some amalgamites topside, I'm going to need every advantage I can get."

He looked away and sighed.

The way his eyes were moving made it clear he was having an internal debate. I could have pushed my agenda further to tip him over the fence, but I knew he'd do what was necessary. Chuck would either trust that I wouldn't use the skill without there being a dire need, or I'd find someone who wouldn't care one way or the other.

And, let's face it, there were plenty of vampires who wouldn't give a shit what I did with the knowledge as long as they got whatever payment they wanted.

"All right, Chief," he said, finally, "I'll do it. But you have to promise me you'll only use it if you have no other choice."

I gave him a serious look.

"You have my word."

"Okay." He motioned to the ground. "Sit down."

I sat, although I wasn't exactly a fan of having dirt all over my suit pants. That was one thing about training in an arena, there was dirt everywhere.

Ah well, at least it wasn't drool or goop.

"Cross your legs," Chuck instructed.

"Are we going to meditate or something?" I asked before complying. "If so, I already know how to calm my mind and clear my thoughts."

His look told me to just shut up and follow instructions.

"Okay, okay," I said, and then crossed my legs.

"Put your hands on your knees, palms up. Touch your thumb to your first finger and let the rest of your fingers relax."

I did.

"You already know how to release your fangs," he continued. "Do so now."

I hated doing it, but after a few moments they slid out to their full length. I could only hope that Rachel wasn't watching from afar because she *loved* the fangs.

"*You know—*" began The Admiral.

"*Quiet!*"

"*Right.*"

"Now," Chuck said in a calm voice, "you need to imagine that your soul is starting to boil."

"Uhhh?"

"It needs to be controlled, though," he was quick to point out. "We're not talking about you being angry or filled with rage. I'm talking about a direct control of your inner essence. It needs to burn."

"Burn," I said with a nod. "Right."

How I was supposed to manage this, I didn't know. It sounded like Chuck wanted me to go through the equivalent of that reproductive pon farr thing that Spock dealt with on the Genesis planet in *Star Trek III*.

Fortunately, I wasn't going through a sexual change.

"I hope not!" agreed The Admiral. I was about to give him a piece of my mind, but he quickly added, *"Shit. Sorry again."*

I growled to myself.

Then I released a long, slow breath and cleared my mind.

The moment everything fell to calmness, I saw a small light in my mind's eye. It was spinning like a vortex.

Vortex!

That had to be my soul. It was white and spinning peacefully.

I needed it to burn.

But how?

My first reaction was to imagine that I was channeling a flame at it, flying from my fingertips. I *was* part mage, after all.

Surprisingly, that worked.

Within seconds, the vortex began to cycle faster and faster, pulling in the burning power spilling towards it from my fingers.

The glow was getting stronger by the minute.

I was beginning to sweat.

That's when I felt it. An acidic rush that poured through my veins, finding its way to my neck, then face, then gums.

My eyes snapped open, smoldering as I glared at Chuck.

"That's it," he said, a worried look covering his face. "If you bite anyone with that, Chief, they'll be under your power, or they'll die."

"Thuper," I said, lisping because my teeth were out.

That killed the mood.

"Fuck."

CHAPTER 17

*I*t honestly wasn't in my best interest to start fighting the valkyries yet, but I had to test out what I'd learned thus far. My main concern was the healing. If it allowed me to sustain a battle against these ladies, it'd certainly be useful against the amalgamites.

In their domain, the valkyries were nearly impossible to kill, but they could be injured. Me, on the other hand? I was rather easily killed when compared to them, especially because they were seriously good at destruction.

"Now remember," I said as I stared across at three rather large warrior chicks, "this is just a mock battle. Nobody wants to be seriously hurt here, right?"

They nodded, but their eyes were cold and filled with wicked intentions.

I gulped.

"Have you all stretched?" I asked.

They furrowed their brows.

"I'm just asking because I know you all don't get a lot of opportunities to fight much anymore. Pulling a hamstring is not..."

I trailed off, and with good reason.

Each of them took a leg and brought it straight up in the air. I'm talking *straight up* so that the bottom of their boots were parallel to the ceiling. They didn't even look the least bit bothered by keeping that pose either.

"*Seriously, man,*" rasped The Admiral, "*I know I'm supposed to shut up and all, but dayyyyum.*"

"*Yeah, okay, I'm with you on that one.*" I then added, "*Still, though, shut up.*"

"*No problem.*"

"*And don't even think about standing at attention right now,*" I warned him.

"*You're no fun.*"

My first inclination was to lift my leg up like they were doing, but I knew damn well that I'd pull a muscle. I was limber, but nothing like these babes.

"Okay," I said, waving at them to stop the we're-so-going-to-kick-your-ass demonstration, "I get it. You can lower your legs now."

They did.

Slowly.

It wasn't exactly a boon to my confidence to see how incredibly controlled they were. But I also knew there was something more to them than simply physical power. They had a level of magic running through their bodies that gave them strength, speed, and that amazing limberness.

I couldn't ask them to shut that down, but if they were

allowed to use it, shouldn't I be allowed to use *all* of my skills?

I wasn't talking about fireballs, ice storms, energy pulses, fangs, claws, and so on, either. I was talking about my *special* brand of magic. The kind that made the ladies shudder with pleasure when I released my energy into them.

"Is everything fair game here?" I asked, just to clarify.

"What do you mean?" Valerie replied from her throne.

I turned to her.

"Well, your warriors are all imbued with magic, right?"

"They are."

"So if they're able to use that magic, does that mean I am allowed to utilize mine as well?"

Valerie shrugged.

"Fine by me."

"I'm talking about my amalgamite sexual energy magic here, Valerie," I added for clarity.

She shrugged and then turned to the three warriors.

"Do any of you have an issue with him pushing sexual energy into you?"

Their heads shook so fast that I felt a breeze.

"Okay, then," I said, knowing damn well that I was going to quickly win this battle. "That should make things easier."

I turned back to my challengers and smiled at them in such a way that their cold eyes changed to excited eyes. They must have spotted my newfound confidence in our impending clash, but that didn't seem to bother them.

"Ready when you are, ladies," I said as I flexed my hands.

Three seconds later, I was lying on the ground, battered and bruised.

I hadn't even seen them twitch. In fact, I didn't even know I'd been hit until the pain began welling up inside me.

It was immediately apparent that fighting three of them at once had been a huge mistake.

"Ouch," I whimpered while trying to untangle my legs.

They'd pretzeled me!

But, wait, wasn't the point of this to use my new skills and magic?

I closed my eyes and sent a healing wave through my body. Everything straightened, except for The Admiral, of course, and I stood back up, brushing off my suit.

Then, I stared back at the three valkyries.

"That was really impressive," I said, stepping over casually while laughing. They relaxed slightly. "If I didn't know any better, I would have said you were able to control time."

I touched the one nearest me and she moaned. With lightning speed, I touched the other two as well. Now, before you go getting up in my face about sending sexual energy through them, you should recall that a) I'd asked if I was allowed to use *my* powers in this fight first, b) they'd all vehemently agreed, and c) I'd only sent enough mojo into them to give them a rush of horniness and nothing more.

But it gave me enough time to go half wolf and start my attack. My hands elongated, my jaw stretched out, and my teeth ached to tear into flesh.

I growled.

I flexed.

I set my eyes to full smolder.

I attacked.

That time I lasted a good seven seconds.

"Okay, okay," I said after healing myself again. "I think I'm going to need to work with the mages next."

"Touch us again first?" asked the closest valkyrie.

Since we weren't in a fight anymore, I felt weird about that. I glanced over at Rachel and she nodded while wearing a wicked grin.

Weirdo.

"Right," I said as I reached out and gave them all another jolt of sexual yum-yum.

CHAPTER 18

Griff, Jasmine, and Rachel all stood across from me, holding looks that spelled they were the masters and I was merely an apprentice. This was the kind of look I was used to seeing from Rachel, so that didn't bother me. It was awkward coming from Griff and Jasmine, though.

"What is the most powerful spell you've utilized thus far?" Griff asked, clearly taking control of the training.

"Uh…I don't know what they're called," I replied, "but I've done some energy stuff and some flames."

He nodded. "Did you feel anything uncomfortable as you were launching these incantations?"

"Not really."

"What did you feel?"

I took a deep breath. "Power, mostly."

All three of them grimaced at that response. Then they looked at each other with concerned faces. It was instantly clear that "power" wasn't the answer they were hoping for.

"So, I'm guessing that's a bad thing?"

"It's not great," Jasmine replied. "There are three types of mages, Ian. Controlled, chaotic, and power."

I chewed my lip. "And because I answered your question with 'power,' that makes me the power type, right?"

"No," answered Rachel. "I'd guess you're chaotic."

I furrowed my brow.

"How does that make any sense?" I asked, feeling confused.

Griff stepped forward, as if called to do a lecture on the subject. He even smoothed out his beard and adjusted his jacket before beginning.

"A mage seeking power," he began, "would choose his answer more carefully. Cleverness and misdirection would be on his side." He looked away for a moment. "They are the most difficult to trace due to their effectiveness at making others believe they are controlled in their thinking."

"Then again," Jasmine was quick to point out, "a fast response like the chief just gave could be a ruse as well."

Griff was nodding as she finished her sentence. He had his right elbow resting on his left arm as he stroked his facial hair thoughtfully.

"I had considered that, too," he replied finally. "The issue I have with the supposition, however, is that Chief Dex has not held these powers long enough to build such thoughtful connections. By way of example," he continued, holding out his hand, "he didn't even know about the three different mage classifications."

"Unless he was faking that too," noted Rachel.

I frowned at her.

"Possible," Griff agreed, "but I don't think so."

"Thank you, Griff," I said, after tearing my irritated look away from Rachel. "At least *one* of you has a little faith in me."

"That's not fair," Rachel retaliated. "I have very little faith in you."

"Oh, well, thanks then..." My head shot up as I realized what she'd done there. She was smiling again. "Nice."

That statement caused an instant tilt in the way Griff was studying me. His eyes squinted and he pursed his lips. A few moments later, he sighed and turned back to Rachel.

"You may be right," he stated.

"What the fuck?" I rasped. "I'm not some power-hungry mage, guys. You know me better than that."

"Said like a true power-hungry mage," Jasmine replied.

"Yep," agreed Rachel.

Griff kept his opinion on my outburst to himself, but I knew what he was thinking. He'd been around the longest and had seen most everything. If any of them knew what kind of mage I was, it'd be him. Actually, you'd think it'd be *me* who knew what kind of mage I was, but...

I turned my attention back to them.

"Does it really matter which of the three I am?" I asked. "I mean, the point of me doing this is to battle the amalgamites, not take over the world."

They glanced back and forth at each other for a few

moments, nodding now and then. This meant they were in direct connection with each other. The connectors didn't work from here to topside, but since we were all within range of each other, the line-of-site linkages functioned just fine.

"The reason it is important to know which type of mage you are," Griff said as all their eyes turned back to me, "is that it determines how we may best train you. If you seek power, we will need to downplay the finer elements of attack spells; if you are chaotic, which we fear you may be, then we will have to focus on control." He paused. "If you were a control type, such as the three of us, this would go much more smoothly."

I scoffed at that remark.

"Wait a second here," I said, nearly laughing, "you're trying to tell me that Rachel is a control mage?"

"Correct," answered Griff as Rachel sneered.

"Well, now I've heard everything."

Rachel took a menacing step forward. "Don't make me kick your ass, Ian."

"And there is my case-in-point," I said with a pompous grin. "She can't even control herself when I'm just ribbing her."

"Ah," Griff said, gently pulling Rachel back. "I see your mental disconnect. Being a control mage has nothing to do with your demeanor. It has to do with your intent."

"You mean like Rachel's intent to kick my ass?"

"When doing magic," Griff clarified, again pulling Rachel back, "a mage may be sinisterly calm, yet still contain the seeds of chaos. Or, as in Ms. Cress's case, filled with animosity while retaining strong control as she enacts spells."

Okay, that was fair. Rachel *was* a hothead, but she was also able to keep her focus in battle like very few people I knew. She'd spout venom, punish the bad guys like there was no tomorrow, and shoot off some pretty heinous spells to render people dead, but her magic was always crafted and controlled.

Actually, it was one of the things that kind of turned me on about her.

"All right," I said, putting my hands up in surrender, "so I'm either a chaos mage or a power one. I'd guess chaos, but maybe I'm fooling myself too. I'm not very good at this stuff, obviously." I shrugged. "Regardless, what does that mean for my training?"

Another session of nods between the three mages ensued. I didn't know why they couldn't just discuss their thoughts aloud. It seemed silly to me. Maybe they had to select the right words or it'd unleash a furious magical demon from my soul or some shit.

I glanced around at the thought.

No, we weren't in the level of demons down here, but they weren't too far away.

Then, I groaned at myself. Even if I was thinking about demons, so what? It wasn't like the mere thought of them would cause a summoning.

Right?

Fuck. I did it again.

Maybe there was a "dumb mage" classification?

"We have discussed it," Griff said at last. "Our plan is to train you as if you are chaotic." I was about to reply, but he held up a finger. "Do note that this will result in you becoming more potent if you turn out to be a power mage, so we will entrust that you shall endeavor to control yourself."

I wanted to ask what would happen if I was unable to control myself, but the serious looks on their faces answered the question for me.

Their collective faces said, "Ian would be a dead power mage."

"Right," was all I said.

CHAPTER 19

The first thing they had me do was practice opening my hands, turning them palm up, and creating small, controlled fireballs.

They weren't powerful enough to do much, but that wasn't the point.

"Good," Griff said supportively. "Float them slowly around, controlling every moment."

"Keep your eyes straight ahead," warned Jasmine. "If you look at them, they'll mesmerize you. That can be deadly."

"Deadly?" I said, raising an eyebrow. "I mean, I guess I could be burned, sure, but deadly?"

Rachel piped up in response. "When you stare at your own magic, it turns in on itself. It'll build and build, feeding on your energy. The visual may not look much different to you, but inside the power is boiling."

"Exactly," agreed Jasmine. "Worse, it grabs hold of your

mind in the same way. Staring for too long will lock you in a loop."

"And that," Griff finished, "is when everything will combust."

Okay, so if I stared at my magic, it grew, and then *boom*. Again, so what? Hadn't I read somewhere that magic didn't impact the one who casts it? Meaning that if I shot an energy beam at my own reflection and it bounced back at me, it wouldn't do anything. This had something to do with the energy signature of the mage matching the energy signature of the magic. If they're the same, they cancel out.

"But it's *my* magic," I said with a tilt of my head. "How can it hurt me?"

"Ah, yes," said Griff with a satisfied nod. Apparently, I had impressed him with my knowledge in this area. At least that was something. "You are speaking of signatures, and you are correct. But this is a different type of explosive release."

I glanced over at the valkyries while fighting *not* to think about...

"*An explosive release,*" finished The Admiral. "*Count me in, brother.*"

I groaned at him.

"The type of impact this causes is one of pure magic," Griff continued. "The spell doesn't strike you as much as it consumes you."

"You mean like a black hole, right?" I asked. They all looked at me. "PBS, guys. You *know* I watch a lot of shows about this stuff."

They didn't respond.

Anyway, I got what they were saying. Admiring your own work too much can backfire on you. In the context of magic, it could be super destructive.

So I looked past the fire I was coaxing to life, controlling it and molding it until it was dripping liquid heat onto the ground around me.

"Okay, stop," commanded Griff.

The flames disappeared.

"Well done," he said, looking taken aback. "Most people require a fair bit of effort to cease once they are so far entrenched."

"Really?" I asked, not expecting an answer. And as expected, I didn't get one. "Okay, so now what?"

"Now we begin casting."

"Sweet," I said.

Rachel smiled at me and walked out to stand in front of me. Her hands began to glow and she put up a small shield.

"Uh…shouldn't you put a little more meat into that forcefield, babe?"

"Won't need it."

I chuckled at her.

"I think you probably will."

"No, she won't," Griff corrected me. "You will only be casting pellet-sized ice and fire spells at her."

"Oh," I replied, deflated.

"It's important for accuracy and control," Jasmine said, giggling. "We've all been through it."

"You may also find that it comes in useful one day," added Griff. "Battling pixies who use other pixies as shields is a great example."

"You've done that?" I asked, my face full of awe.

His response was a deadened look that told me he didn't want to talk about it. That meant it had happened in the old war.

There must have been a lot that went on back then.

Sadly, I'd never learn about it because those who fought in that war were very tightlipped about what they'd experienced.

I supposed in fifty years or so there'd be some upstart who'd want to hear all about the adventures of Ian Dex and Las Vegas PPD as we fought against a bunch of ubers over the last year. I'd probably be annoyed at being asked about it all the time, too.

"Right," I said with a sigh as I looked over at Rachel's pathetic shield. "So, ice pellets?"

"And fire, too," replied Jasmine.

CHAPTER 20

The next twenty minutes consisted of me firing mini spells at mini shields. It was tedious, but I'd be lying if I didn't admit that it was also fun as hell.

I could see this being an awesome way for mages to play a form of laser tag.

Magic tag? Spell tag? MagiTag, maybe?

Every now and then I'd purposely let one of the little spells go slightly off target, striking Rachel in her tender spot. Her initial reaction was an intense glare, but then I got a direct connect saying, "Do it again…please."

Weirdo.

Griff appeared impressed with my abilities. He kept saying things like, "I've never seen such accuracy in a beginner," and "You're *certain* you've not done this before?" Obviously, I hadn't, but he was having a tough time believing that.

"Just a moment," said finally Griff. "Rachel, move to that side a bit farther, and Jasmine, step over there."

They both split apart but kept their shields at the ready.

Griff turned to me but then turned back. "Extend your shields, please."

They did, though Rachel left the center of her shield open. Griff rolled his eyes at her.

"Ian," my mage master said, "I want you to try and strike both shields in their centers as best you can. You will be firing at the same time with both hands, and I'd ask that you increase the number of spells cast as well. It should get to the point where you must be fully engaged."

Seemed easy enough to me.

"You mean like this?"

I unleashed a barrage of pellets at Jasmine and Rachel, striking the center of their shields with ease. To make it more of a challenge, I began swapping fire and ice realtime. I even took to crossing my arms, firing left with my right and right with my left.

I didn't miss even once.

As far as being fully engaged went, I wasn't. To be honest, I couldn't imagine that I could ramp up enough to have this take over my mind.

A quick glance over at Griff showed that he was beside himself.

"Everything okay?" I asked, no longer looking at where I was firing. "You seem surprised by this?"

In response, he furrowed his brow seriously and stared back at the two ladies I was firing upon. A few nods later, they both started moving around, making for non-stationary targets.

It took a little more effort to keep up with them now that they were moving, but I managed just fine, missing only a couple of times.

"Remarkable," Griff marveled, waving at me to stop.

I did.

Based on his reaction, and the looks on the faces of Rachel and Jasmine, it was clear that I shouldn't have been able to do what I had just done.

It seemed pretty easy to me.

"Power mage," Jasmine stated, stepping back over as she lowered her shield. "Never seen a chaotic who could do that."

"Nor I," agreed Griff. He gave me a stern eye. "You must endeavor to maintain your control or the power will consume you."

"Right," I said, nodding. "I get it. Don't look at my own spells. We've been over that already, Griff. I don't need to be told twice."

"He's talking about the magic in general, Ian," Rachel said, appearing as serious as Griff. It wasn't often that Rachel got that look, so I was immediately put on edge. "This isn't a joke, babe," she added. "There are only a few power mages out there, because they're usually..." She trailed off, glancing away from me.

"Killed," I finished for her. "Swell. So how do I stop the power from taking me over?"

Griff looked into my eyes. "Only use it when absolutely necessary. Do everything you can to avoid it." He gestured around. "Even the training we've just done may have been unwise."

"Oh, come on, Griff," I said with a laugh. "Don't you think you guys are being a little overly dramatic here?" I stepped back and put my hands out. "It's me, Ian. I'm the guy who sleeps with..." I glanced at Rachel and swallowed hard. "...uh, I mean *used* to sleep with succubi. I'm a womanizer, I drink a lot, I giggle at dick jokes, I buy expensive toys...I'm basically a teenager stuck deep in a man's body." I squinted. "Okay, that sounded disturbingly wrong, but my recognizing that only further solidifies how immature I am. You can't honestly see *me* as being some power mage who could ever be serious enough to rule the world?"

They didn't appear convinced.

Fine, so their worry was genuine.

That meant mine had to be as well.

Truth be told, I preferred not using magic anyway, so if I could figure a way out of a situation without employing its use, that would be all the better.

I took a deep breath and slowly released it.

"Okay," I assured them, "I'll do my best to avoid using magic wherever possible."

"Good," was Griff's only response.

"So what's next?"

"Nothing," he said soberly. "You are frankly more advanced than the three of us put together at this point. The only additional information we could provide would do no more than make you wish to utilize your magic as much as possible. And, as I've already stated, that would be unwise."

Jasmine and Griff turned and walked back toward the others.

Rachel stayed with me.

"You okay?" she asked.

"I'm fine," I replied, feeling a little irked. "The fact is that I was expecting a bit more help from you guys. Shooting at shields is…well, more fun than I expected, but I don't see how it's going to help me stand up against mages like you guys."

She gave me a look that conveyed she thought me an idiot.

"Are you being serious?" she chided. "Ian, if you hadn't been firing pellets, you could have easily killed me and Jasmine. We wouldn't have had a chance."

"You had your shields up."

"Granted," she acquiesced, "but a power mage can strip…" She stopped as her face went pale.

I tilted my head and squinted at her.

"Something tells me that you didn't mean 'strip' as in take off my clothes, Rachel." I felt my eyes smoldering slightly. "What do you mean?"

"I…"

"Tell me," I commanded in such a way that I felt magical energy coming through the words. She shuddered, signaling it *was* magic. "Whoa," I said, shaking myself and then blinking a few times. "I just compelled you, didn't I?"

She nodded as if terrified.

I didn't like that look.

"I'm sorry," I said, taking her in my arms. "I didn't know what I was doing."

"That's the point, Ian," she said, shaking. "You have to be careful. Even the little amount of training you've been through has opened doors that should have remained closed. If you don't control it—"

"You guys will have to kill me," I interrupted.

"Or die trying," she added.

CHAPTER 21

Next up was Warren and wizardry. I had the feeling this was going to be a struggle because I wasn't exactly the patient type and Warren was notoriously slow at everything.

But, I needed to learn and he needed to teach, so I set some ground rules right from the start.

"Look, Warren," I said, "I know being a wizard means you have to be meticulous and all that, but we don't have a lot of time. That means we're going to need to skip pointless descriptions and processes. We have to focus and get right into it. Cool?"

"No."

"Good, because…" I frowned. "What?"

"No," he repeated, setting his feet. "I'm not going to just give you a couple of pointers and walk away. Wizardry is serious stuff, man."

"I…uh…" I blinked a few times in disbelief and repeated, "No?"

He sighed.

"Chief," he said, "I know you think I'm basically a waste of space."

I went to reply but couldn't find the words.

"And that's cool," Warren continued, "but I'm on the PPD because I'm good at what I do. Any wizard who has ample skill realizes how important it is to take it slow. Rushing wizardry is like jumping off an edge without first checking to see how far you're going to be falling."

"Why would you jump off an edge at all?" I pondered. "I suppose if you had on a parachute or something..."

He was eyeing me now.

The fact was I *didn't* think Warren was a waste of space. Slower than a sloth trying to fuck a snail? Yes. But he was a solid wizard who had contributed to saving my team more than once over our time together. If I had the stats in front of me, they'd probably label Warren as the *most* utilized piece of the puzzle in the PPD.

It wouldn't matter if I told him that, though. There were too many instances of me being short about how long it took for him to do even what appeared to be simple tasks.

He was methodical.

He was exacting.

He was slow.

In a nutshell, Warren was a wizard.

Did that mean he *never* screwed up? Not at all. But when he did make mistakes, they were often not as horrific as they could be. And, to his point, a wizard making mistakes could be catastrophic.

"Fair enough," I said, bowing my head slightly, "but

that being the case, and knowing the kind of time constraints we're faced with here, what can you teach me that will be useful and efficient?"

"Runes," he replied without hesitation. That was a rare thing. "Not creating them," he amended while holding up a finger, "but rather reading and diffusing them."

I gave him a funny look.

"Aren't there, like, thousands of designs, though?"

"Billions," he corrected me. Then he looked away. "Probably more. They're all individualized by the wizard to some extent, but they share commonalities that make them easily read, if you know how."

"Ah, cool."

"Diffusing them, however, is quite a bit more complex."

He dropped to the ground and pulled out a little stick that he used as a wand. It wasn't a traditional wand, at least not like the kind you see in the movies. There was no store that wizards rushed off to in order to buy them. Warren had once stated that he'd found his while hiking through a forest in the northwest part of the United States. I never got into the specifics as to *why* he'd selected this particular stick, because I never really cared, but now that I was learning this stuff…

"Question for you," I said, interrupting his drawing. "How come you chose *that* stick instead of all the others?"

"It's a wand," he said, appearing offended on its behalf.

"Oh, right," I replied. "My apologies to the stick…erm, wand."

He turned back to his work. "It called to me."

"Ah," I muttered. "That makes sense."

"No, it doesn't, man," he mused. "It doesn't make any sense at all, which is why I selected it to be my wand."

"Were you smoking something at the time?" I asked.

"Probably."

"Does it still call to you?" I ventured, thinking someone needed to tell Warren he was supposed to take *all* prescribed medications, not just the pretty ones. "Do you have conversations with it?"

He gave me a sidelong glance. "Of course."

"Hmmm." I sniffed in and asked, "Am I going to need a talking stick, too, or can I do whatever needs doing without one?"

"Again, man," he said, looking annoyed, which was something I wasn't used to seeing with Warren, "it's a wand, not a stick."

"Well, technically—"

"And you should have a wand, yes." He continued his drawing. "You can decipher without one, but diffusing may be more difficult unless you just use your mage abilities. That can backfire, though, depending on how clever the wizard was who built the runes."

That didn't sound fun. I'd already suffered being shocked by fucking runes more often than I cared to recall. They hurt like hell. I didn't even want to think about how bad it could be if I cast a spell at one and it backfired on me.

"That could be a problem, then," I breathed.

"Why?"

"Because I highly doubt there are any talking sticks around here, Warren," I responded, and then caught myself. "Sorry, wands."

"You've always got me, pal," The Admiral suggested.

"Oh yeah, that's going to look great," I replied with a grunt. *"We're in the midst of trouble and I have to whip you out and diffuse a rune."*

"That'd be badass, man!" The Admiral seemed rather enthusiastic regarding the prospect. *"We'd be legendary. Think about it. Who else in all of the world of wizardry has a dick as a wand?"*

"You'll just have to use your finger," Warren stated after a short pause. "It's not ideal, man, but it'll work."

"Even though it doesn't talk to me?"

His look told me I was being an idiot.

'Professor Warren' was not nearly as laidback as 'subordinate Warren.'

Two minutes later, his rune was completed. It didn't seem very complex. There were blue spokes running from a tiny green circle that sat at the center. The spokes attached to a larger red circle that encased everything. Some of the sections between the spokes were filled with a dark yellow color, the rest with blue. All in all, it looked like something you'd buy at a craft show.

"Do you know what this is?" he asked me as he stood up and pointed at the rune.

"A rune?"

That response garnered me another look.

I cleared my throat.

"No," I said, which was surprising since I had been able to read the runes by Tommy Rocker's without a problem. Maybe I'd lost that ability already or something? "I don't know what kind of rune it is," I admitted. "Did you do something special to hide it?"

"Yes."

"Oh," I said, scratching my neck. "I'm guessing not all wizards do that?"

"Most do," he said. "It depends on how difficult they want to make things. Sometimes it's better that people know what they're dealing with so they stay away."

"Ah, right." I glanced at it again. "Okay, I give up...what is it?"

"Shocker rune."

I stepped back.

"I hate those fucking things," I said, staring at it. "They hurt like hell."

"Yep," he agreed. "That's what they're supposed to do, man." He pointed again. "But what do you see when you look at the rune?"

I described the colors, the circles, and the tendrils.

Then, I said, "Hey, I thought Shockers were made with integrated x-patterns, not tendrils?"

"You can design them however you want, dude," Warren commented. "The design you see with your eyes is what you need to use in order to unravel a rune. It's what you see with your magic that defines what a rune actually represents."

Okay, that was trippy.

"Huh?"

"Think of it like a present," he explained. "What you're seeing there is the wrapping paper. It's the box that holds the truth of the rune underneath. Each box is different, but the underlying rune is either identical or highly similar to any Shocker that any wizard would create." He pushed his hair out of his eyes. "There *are* different

Shockers, sure, but they all share the same basic mechanics." He pointed again. "Now, look at it with your magic instead of with your eyes."

"Right, okay," I said, turning my attention back to the rune. After about five seconds I asked, "How do I do that, again?"

"Look *through* the wrapping, man," he instructed while pushing out his hands. "See beyond the shell. Dig deeper. Push past the layers of the onion. Split it down to the deepest recesses of—"

"Warren," I interrupted, "I get it."

"Ah, okay."

I calmed my breathing a little and stared at the rune. At first, nothing happened. It was just a pretty little design like the ones I'd seen before. Not as intricate, obviously, but Warren hadn't really spent a lot of time fleshing this one out.

Then I saw it.

It was almost like looking at an x-ray.

I was seeing the 'bones' of the rune. They were too dim at first, but after a few seconds, the details started to brighten. Pretty soon the wrapping faded and I was looking at the core of the damn thing.

That's when I scoffed and let out a laugh.

"You're fucking kidding me, right?"

Warren looked concerned. "What?"

"It literally says 'Shocker' right on it," I stated while pointing.

"So?"

"Did you put that on there for my benefit or something?"

"No," he answered seriously. "That's how runes are managed."

"They're *named?*"

"Of course. How else would you do it?"

"Come on, man!" I was shaking my head uncontrollably. "That's laughable, and those runes I saw at Tommy Rocker's weren't named like that."

Finally, he relented and smiled.

"Oh, my God," I said, staring at my resident wizard with wide eyes. "You just played a joke on me, Warren!"

"Sorry, Chief," he giggled. "It's something we do to all new wizards."

I suppose I should have expected that. It was just like how we razzed junior officers now and then. Honestly, I kind of appreciated it after the whole 'power mage' revelation from Griff, Jasmine, and Rachel.

"Funny."

"Thanks," he said.

I shook my head. "It's so weird that I could just read them at Tommy Rocker's, but not here."

He reached over and did a couple of things to the rune. When he pulled back, I could see it perfectly.

"Yeah, it was like that!" I exclaimed while pointing.

"Because whoever made those runes didn't block them," he pointed out.

He fiddled with it again.

It clouded back over.

"Ah, right."

"Anyway, when you have to go through a protected rune you'll need to look for the multiple sets of switches that are in the middle of the rune. Each one has a set. How they're configured determines what the rune will do."

"So they're like dip switches?"

He looked at me appraisingly. "Exactly."

"Is there a key somewhere that tells me what each setting is all about?"

"It's in here," he answered, tapping his first finger against my forehead. "Stare at the settings for a few moments and the answer will reveal itself."

Sure enough, it did.

It wasn't so much a visual image as it was the general feeling that I *knew* what the rune was engineered to do. That was actually pretty cool.

"Great," I said, feeling at least somewhat accomplished. "Now, I was able to diffuse those non-protected ones without a fuss, but how do I diffuse a protected one?"

"Very carefully," he replied.

CHAPTER 22

With the basics of runes out of the way, I only needed to get some pixie training under my belt. I knew Turbo *wasn't* the pixie for the job, but he had skills I might need.

"But I'm not good with using Pixie Dust, Chief," he complained while buzzing in front of me at eye-height. "I can use it, but I never really excelled at it."

"I'm not worried about that, Turbo," I replied in a calm voice. "I'm more concerned about the other skills you possess."

"You mean foul language and name-calling?" he asked, plucking at his PPD cap. "I'm *okay* at that, but I'd say you're probably better at it than I am."

That was true. I'd heard him spew out a few choice names now and then, like when we'd busted him out of Red's trunk, but if he and I were to go head to head in a Pixie *Joke-Off* contest, I'd annihilate him.

"I'm talking about your ability with technology," I explained. "I suck at that stuff."

"You want me to teach you tech?" he asked, his little face scrunched up. "Why?"

"Because I may need it when I'm facing those amalgamites, Turbo."

"I don't see how," he said, shaking his head. "But even if you did, there's no way I could teach you everything I know without having a couple of years to do it."

One of the primary issues I had with Turbo, and a few other techies I'd worked with over the years, was that they took things too literally. Obviously he couldn't teach me everything he knew, but I didn't need to know everything.

"I get that, Turbo," I said without inflection, "but there has to be some type of wisdom you can impart, maybe?"

"Oh, sure, sure," he said, flying back and forth in front of me as if pacing in the air. "Let's see." He snapped his fingers and pointed at me. "Ah hah! Okay, so those Netherworld emails where a guy says that his uncle died and he's going to split a couple million with you if you give him your bank info…those are fake."

I rubbed my temples.

"No good?" he asked.

"No."

"Hmmm." He snapped his fingers again. "Don't ever give your password to someone online!"

"Seriously?" I said, staring at him. "Everyone knows that, Turbo."

"Somehow I doubt that," he replied. Then, he gave me a hopeful look. "Don't take any wooden nickels?"

My initial thought was to guesstimate how far I could

launch a pixie from my current location, but I held myself in check. He was clearly doing his best here. He just didn't really have much to offer me.

That's when he rubbed his fingers together, held his nose for a second, and then held up a tiny key.

He gazed at it lovingly.

"I suppose I could just give you my universal access key," he said with some hesitation. "It might help."

I took it from him, noting that it was only the size of a fingernail in my hands.

"What's it do?" I asked.

"Hold it up to any door that has an electronic lock and it'll open it."

I gawked at him. "No shit?"

"It might take a little while to work as it seeks to crack the code of the door," he explained, "but I've never seen it fail."

"Sweet!"

"But you have to be careful with it," he warned. "It wasn't easy to build that and I don't want to have to do it again."

"Oh, right," I said, looking for the best place to put it. Then I recalled how he brought it out. "Uh…where did you keep it?"

"It's got a magical element to it," he replied. "You just rub your fingers and hold your nose and it'll disappear into your flesh."

I frowned. "Why do you have to hold your nose?"

"Because I didn't want the key to come out whenever I rubbed my fingers together, so I added an element to the sequence when I was working with the mage who helped me."

I glanced over my shoulder at my three mages. My assumption was that Griff was the one who aided Turbo since he was most often working with the pixie.

"Okay," I said.

Then I began rubbing the key between my fingers as I held my nose. About three seconds in, the key disappeared. I didn't feel a thing and I couldn't see the key hiding under the skin or anything. As a test, I rubbed my fingers again as I held my nose. The key came back.

"Dude," I said with glittering eyes, "that's fucking sweet. I'm loving this thing!"

Turbo whimpered.

CHAPTER 23

The three valkyries had come back onto the field. They were all standing right next to me, clearly hoping I'd give them another touch of yum-yum.

"Hello, ladies," said The Admiral.

He was clearly into it. Wasn't he always? But I had other business on my mind.

I'd gained enough knowledge from my training to hopefully extend my chances against the valkyries. I didn't need to win, but getting past ten seconds would be nice. And while it was clear that using my magical love-touch had been somewhat helpful, I had the feeling it wouldn't be as effective the second time around. I mean, it'd certainly give them the tingles, but the ladies wouldn't let it cloud their judgment now that they knew better.

Besides, it wasn't like I was going to use that spell on someone without their consent. That'd be beyond wrong. Plus, I would be facing my 'brothers,' so...ew.

"Agreed," confirmed The Admiral.

To make this even more challenging, it was pretty clear that my use of magic was *not* the best idea. I didn't think I'd ever forget the look on Rachel's face when my words compelled her. It frankly made me sick.

Small bursts of magic were probably okay for healing and such, but full launches of mayhem? No.

So that left me back at square one against these three.

Unless...

I moved back away from them and set my hands to glowing.

There was little doubt that Griff, Jasmine, and Rachel were all giving me dubious stares at the moment, but I knew what I was doing.

Maybe.

I lifted my hands up and began making those same little magic pellets that I'd made before. They wouldn't do any damage, of course, but that wasn't the point. My goal was to use them as a diversion.

A few pellets raced from my hands, shooting straight up so the valkyries wouldn't think I was starting my attack.

Their eyes followed each one as if they were watching a light show.

Perfect.

With their attention elsewhere, I began a slow morph into partial wolf form. Once I felt my clothing start to strain under the pressure of my change, I stopped and began to gradually circle behind the valkyries.

It was more challenging to keep their attention on my magic since I was moving around them, but I quickly learned that I could curve the path of the pellets. They zipped straight out, arced left, and then flew right up to join the others. That could prove majorly useful in battle, especially if I could manage that with larger spells.

Once I was in position, I grinned to myself knowing that I'd figured them out.

I flicked my wrist, causing the pellets to all explode in a dazzling array of colors.

The ladies clapped their hands just as I launched myself at their backs.

That was when I realized that these chicks were even better at knowing their arena than I was at knowing my condo.

One hand snaked back and grabbed me by the throat, stopping me dead in my tracks, another hand punched me in the stomach, and yet another punched me in the head. Three hands, three different warrior mamas.

I hadn't stood a chance.

If you counted the start of the magic show, though, I'd lasted nearly a minute. But if we were just measuring the actual physical part of the fight, the only part that genuinely mattered, I don't even think I hit three seconds.

That alone was enough to piss me off.

Seeing three valkyries standing in front of me with crossed arms and smug faces only made it worse.

But what *really* sent me into a complete rage were the laughs from my crew.

Not cool.

The animosity inside me welled up to a point where it burned. Not like a soul-burning type of thing that Serena had me do, but rather a pit of pure anger. I knew I should have put a damper on it, but I was so fucking frustrated that I decided to let it flow.

A howl escaped my lips as the pain racked my body.

I'd gone full werewolf, and that shit hurt.

Finally, the pain subsided and the world became something entirely different than I'd ever experienced.

The smells in the air were unfathomable. I picked up pheromones, dirt, breath, sweat, and even heartbeats. Yes, I realize that sounds strange, but I could actually smell the beating of each heart in that room.

I was also much bigger than before. I knew this because I was looking eye to eye with my three opponents, and they weren't exactly short.

My muscles bulged and my teeth ached for flesh.

There was no hesitation this time.

I launched at the nearest valkyrie and bit her arm.

Hard.

She grunted and clobbered me on top of my head, but I refused to let go. The taste of her blood was almost orgasmic.

Whipping my head back and forth, I fought to tear the limb right from her person.

Just when I thought I would succeed, her two warrior pals came to her aid and I felt a sudden whirlwind of activity.

There was painful cracking, pathetic yelping, horrific shrieking, and unholy squealing filling the arena...all from my lips. Or was it maw?

It seemed like an eternity of anguish before the world finally settled.

I was completely lost.

My brain was not functioning right at all.

I heard a voice yelling at me, imploring me to do something, but I was still fighting through the fog.

Straight in front of my eyes was dirt.

Whatever they'd done to me, it hadn't been even slightly fun. The pain had been beyond belief, even worse than what I'd felt going full wolf, but it seemed to be slowly subsiding.

That voice screamed to me again. I just couldn't make out what it was saying or where it was coming from. It was like hearing a dull echo in a massive underground chamber.

My spine felt curved.

That was odd.

The pounding in my head gradually relaxed as my body fought to heal itself. I wasn't exactly in a position to use magic, after all.

Speaking of positions, I was having a difficult time comprehending how my hind leg was resting on the back of my head.

And that's when my mind cleared enough to allow me to hear The Admiral swearing at me.

"Dude, get your fucking mouth off me!"

Son of a bitch.

The valkyries had used my doggie form and stuck me in a full lip-lock with The Admiral.

I untangled myself, nearly vomiting in the process.

"It's about fucking time," The Admiral complained. *"That was horrible, man. No means NO, remember?"*

The laughs were radiating through the room, but I no longer felt anger. It was more like disgust.

Unfortunately...or maybe fortunately, based on what the valkyries had done to me, I began losing my werewolf form.

"I'm honestly going to need therapy," The Admiral sulked. *"I just can't even begin to tell you how terrible that was."*

I didn't reply. I was too focused on getting my mind back in order. This wasn't easy because the wolf-transition shit apparently messed you up pretty good. Felicia had warned me about that, but I guess I didn't anticipate how bad it could actually be.

If she had to go through this every time she changed over, I'd have to be more understanding about her mood swings in the future.

"I don't think I'll ever be able to have sex again, man."

It took some effort, but I got to my feet and shook my head, nearly falling over in the process.

"What the hell just happened?" I mumbled, my ears ringing with each word.

"You attacked us as a full wolf," said one of the valkyries.

They were all staring down at The Admiral, though.

"My eyes are up here, ladies," I said. Two of them jolted and glanced up, looking somewhat ashamed. The other didn't seem to care what I thought about her staring at my middle part. "Anyway, what happened after I attacked you?"

"We retaliated."

"They stuck me in your mouth, man," The Admiral whined. *"I'll never be the same again."*

That wasn't necessarily a bad thing. Not the part about

him being stuck in my mouth. That *was* bad. I meant the part about him never being the same again.

I looked down to find that my suit was completely ruined.

I pulled the ripped sleeves off and kicked away what was left of my pants. That left me stark naked, except for my red tie and the collar of my dress shirt. I guess my legs and butt had grown so much during the transition that even my boxers had been shredded. That seemed unlikely, though. I glanced up at the valkyries and noted the one who was staring at my junk was also spinning my undies around with her index finger.

Nice.

So there I was, essentially nude in front of everyone.

"Honestly, dude," The Admiral said with a defeated sigh, *"this is one illness that will never fade."*

Valerie stood up from her throne and began walking across the field toward us.

"The damage caused is permanent," lamented The Admiral. *"There's just no returning from something that horrific. I'm done for."*

Valerie's three soldiers came to attention, taking a single step backward as their leader approached. The one holding my boxers had tucked them into her leather belt. My assumption was she wanted to keep them. I didn't want to know why.

"We may as well put up an 'out of business' sign," The Admiral continued his tirade, *"because it's really, truly, deplorably that bad."*

Valerie walked around me, looking me up and down the entire time.

"*I'll never be the same again, man,*" my dick moaned. "*I'll just never be the same.*"

"Your training is done," Valerie declared in a stern voice. "We will now discuss the various methods by which you will pleasure every single one of us."

"*I'm cured!*"

CHAPTER 24

Not only did we discuss it, we enacted a few of the seedier scenes from the roleplaying that was suggested by the valkyries.

My favorite was the one where I was the king and they were all members of my harem.

I'd made Warren the court jester.

He was not pleased.

Griff and Chuck had gone elsewhere, deciding not to participate, for obvious reasons.

Two hours in and I was exhausted.

As if fighting a battle wasn't difficult enough against these ladies, sexing with them—while amazing—was like waging war with your naughty bits.

Don't get me wrong here. I *wasn't* complaining. In fact, I'd go as far as to say that it was by far the best sex I'd ever had in my life, and that included the succubus orgy I'd attended before joining the force. I felt bad putting Rachel as third in my list of all-time greats, but she couldn't possibly compete with a harem of succubi and another of valkyries. Fortunately, she knew that. Her smile was so painfully wide that it was clear I was no longer in her first place position either...assuming I had been before.

Once we were all spent, Griff and Chuck rejoined the group, looking rather disheveled themselves.

"That was far better than we had anticipated, Ian Dex," Valerie cooed, still swooning. My sex-touch would do that to a lady. "I daresay that was even better than when the gods visited so many millennia ago."

"Gods?" I asked, furrowing my brow.

"Yes," she replied. "Zeus, Odin, Aegir, Ganesa, Poseidon—"

"You are mixing various mythologies there, my dear," Griff pointed out.

Valerie turned to him with bright eyes.

"Technically, I'm mixing *human* mythologies," she replied. "The reality of the gods is different than the stories that have been told. Some of the gods carry different names, depending on the society they visited, but are actually the same person. The only true differences come from the fact that there were multiple cultures experiencing them."

Griff said, "Hmmm." He then wagged his finger at her. "That is quite fascinating. I would thoroughly enjoy a solid banter on the subject at some point, should the opportunity avail itself."

"It would be my pleasure," Valerie replied with a genuine smile.

Everyone was busily getting dressed again, except for

me. I could only put my tie back on, and I didn't even bother with the piece of my dress shirt that remained.

The Admiral was back in full spirits, but he did request that we never mention what happened again. He insisted that if we just forgot about it, buried the memory, and act like it was naught but a terrible dream, we would eventually recover fully.

I agreed.

"Chief," said Chuck, his eyes locked on my dangling rope as if he were in shock by the size of it, "what the hell do you feed that thing?"

"Women," I replied without hesitation.

He jolted and looked up at me, blinking.

"Oh, no!" he said quickly. "I wasn't implying that…" He looked away. "Right."

Griff patted his arm in understanding.

I turned around, walked up to the chick who had my boxers, and put my hand out. She pouted but finally relented and gave them back to me.

Now I had a tie and boxers. It wasn't much, but it was better than being fully nude.

"What's the plan?" asked Rachel, still glowing from the mind-blowing sexcapade.

"I have to speak with Valerie alone," I replied. "There are some questions I have regarding the levels here. Since none of you have traversed them, you're not allowed to hear the secrets. It's in the rules."

Rachel tilted her head in such a way that implied she wasn't sure if she believed me or not, but she eventually shrugged and walked away.

I took Valerie by the hand and led her a good distance away from everyone else.

"You do know that your words were untrue just then, yes?" the Amazonian woman asked me.

"Yeah, I know, but I had to speak with you alone and that was the only way I could think of that wouldn't arouse suspicion."

She glanced over her shoulder.

"Why would there be any suspicion?"

"Because, Valerie," I said, feeling like a heel for what I was about to say, "I need to leave them here as I go topside and deal with the people who are hunting me."

She stood at full height and crossed her arms as she stared down at me. Clearly, she was no more fond of my plan than my crew would be if they'd known the truth.

"It is unwise for you to walk into the belly of the beast without assistance, Ian Dex."

"That's probably true," I agreed, "but I've rarely been accused of being wise, Valerie."

She grimaced. "Why do this?"

"Because I don't want them to die," I replied, staring into her eyes. "You saw me on the field of battle today. While I was no match for your warriors, do you think that any of them in that group over there are a match for me?"

"Not even together," she answered, lowering her arms in defeat. "You have become very powerful since your first visit here. If you had fully utilized your magic, I fear that not even my three soldiers could have contained you."

"Exactly," I agreed, even though I found that incredibly challenging to believe. "So now think about the fact that there are four more of me topside right now."

I looked past her and stared at my crew. Yeah, it would piss them off something fierce when they learned I'd left them behind, but better that than all of them pushing up daisies. Some of them were immortal, yes, but only as it related to living in normalcy. Wooden shards striking a vampire heart erased that immortality pretty quickly. Killing werewolves, mages, and wizards wasn't all that difficult either, if you had the strength and the know-how. And pixies? Simple, assuming you could catch them.

"You *do* realize that not even you could manage to succeed in battle against four who are your equals?" Valerie questioned.

"Normally, yes," I answered, "but I don't think they are my equals."

Granted, everyone reported seeing my 'brothers' sporting fangs and doing magic, but it couldn't have been to the level I was at right now. If it had been, they'd have blown right through my team's defenses and taken, or killed, everyone in a matter of minutes. Probably sooner.

"Still," she stated after a few moments of silence, "your friends have a right to die by your side, Ian Dex. It is not up to you to decide their fate."

"I'm their chief, Valerie," I countered. "It's *absolutely* up to me to decide their fate."

She slightly bowed to me.

"Well said, Ian Dex," she remarked as one leader to another. "Very well said."

CHAPTER 25

After we had agreed on our story, Valerie closed her eyes and a thin glow could be seen where her lids pressed together. Finally, she opened them and gave me a nod.

"My soldiers have been informed of our plan," she stated. "Some were unhappy, but all will follow my commands and keep the truth hidden."

"Cool," I said as I reached out and touched her hand. "I really appreciate you doing this for me…and for my team, too."

We walked back to the group. I took the time to put on a serious face and to build my angst. If I played it too aloof, they'd know what was going on. That was especially true of Rachel. She could read me like a book.

Which reminded me…

"You keep your mouth shut, got it?" I instructed The Admiral, knowing how easily Rachel could overhear our discussions.

"*Of course I will,*" he replied, sounding miffed. "*And next time just ask, pal. You don't have to be a douche about it, you know.*"

"Uh, Chief," Chuck started as we approached, "about before. I was—"

"It's okay, Chuck," I replied, patting him on the shoulder. "I know you weren't implying anything."

"Actually, I kind of was, which is why I feel bad about it."

"*Ew,*" rasped The Admiral.

"Oh," I said and then cleared my throat. "Well, let's just call it water under the bridge, Chuck. Cool?"

"Cool," he said, adjusting his hat.

With a nod, I stepped out and stood before the entire team. They were all glowing slightly, which made sense seeing what we'd just been through. Leaving them behind was going to be rough on both them and me, but they'd be able to play some more down here, and as long as my story held together, they wouldn't know I was going topside anyway.

I just had to be smooth about it.

"Valerie and I just had a conversation regarding the various levels of this place," I started. "I know you've all been to the lowest level before, which is why I can share this tidbit of information with you." I gave a moment for that to sink in. "It seems that the basilisk has the ability to put controls on my mind, but only insofar as I allow it."

"So?" asked Rachel, looking concerned.

"It means I can ask him to limit how far the magic can take me, Rachel," I explained. "That would give me the ability to cast spells only strong enough that the power won't overtake my mind."

"That would be ideal, actually," Griff affirmed. "My concern is knowing what the basilisk will request in return."

"Multiple things," I replied. "Each of which can be retrieved by going to the other zones. It will take some time, though."

"But—" began Griff.

"Plus, Basil owes me a favor," Valerie lied on my behalf, using the basilisk's chosen name. Well, at least I assumed it was a lie. "And seeing as how I do not wish to lose Ian Dex, I shall spend that favor to get him what is needed."

I gave her a sad smile and nodded. That wasn't playacting either. I genuinely felt sincerity for how much the valkyries had helped. I wanted to believe there was more to it than merely sex, but I had the feeling there wasn't…at least not yet.

That's when I locked my eyes onto Rachel's and direct-connected to her.

"Are you okay?" I asked, speaking specifically about the sex. *"As I've said before, there's a big difference between fantasy and reality, babe."*

"It was amazing," she replied, her eyes sparkling. *"Seeing you pleasuring them all was such a turn on. I could seriously watch that every day. Also, I found it beyond hot to play with them myself!"*

"Oooookay," I replied, unsure of how I should feel about those admissions. *"We'll have to see about that. Anyway, for now, I need you to stay here and keep the team*

occupied. If that means more playing with the valkyries, that's fine by me."

"What about Warren?" she asked.

"If you mean you want to play with Warren, then no fucking way," I replied flatly. *"Remember, I didn't ask to bone these chicks. You asked me to do that."*

"Babe, relax," she said before I could go on a verbal rampage. *"I was talking about letting him stand in your place with the valkyries while you're gone."*

"Oh, right. Sorry." I had to hold back a laugh at the thought of Warren replacing me, though. Okay, yes, I had quite an ego when it came to pleasing the ladies. Then again, he had spent the night with Felicia, Jasmine, and Serena. Maybe there was more to this wizard than met the eye. He was stuck in the jester's outfit while I was king, after all. I shrugged. *"Yeah, sure, that's cool, as long as his magic wand doesn't touch you."*

Before she could reply, I clapped my hands and brought everyone's attention back to me.

"Okay, so that's it then. I'll probably be gone for a while as I work through this." I stared off for a moment, working to add some dramatic effect. "Hopefully, I'll be back soon enough. It feels like we've been away from the Strip too long as it is." The fact was that we'd been flying blind without the ability to speak with anyone topside. "The sooner I get started, the sooner I'll be back."

At least that much was true, except for the supposition that I'd be returning.

That was a promise I couldn't make.

CHAPTER 26

Valerie targeted my office and sent me back topside. One of the nice things about working with people in the nine levels under the Badlands was that they could pinpoint your return.

It would have been bad to show up somewhere in the middle of the Strip wearing nothing but boxers and a red tie. This was especially true because I was carrying Boomy with me as well. No, I didn't really need him at this point in time. My current skills were plenty deadly all on their own, but I had to stay away from the magic as much as possible. I also had the skeleton key that Turbo had lent me. That was infused in my finger so nobody would be able to spot it.

There wasn't a full suit in my office, but there were a pair of slacks, a button-up shirt, socks, and some basic black shoes. It didn't exactly ring 'Ian,' though. Still, it was better than walking around naked. There hadn't been enough time to go back to my condo and get a full ensemble. Besides, who was to say that my 'brothers' weren't waiting there for me?

"*Is that you, puddin'?*" asked Lydia as I pulled on my shoes.

"Hey, baby," I replied, trying to keep cool. "*Just got back from reintegration. Still waiting on the others. Anything happen while I was gone?*"

"*No,*" she replied. "*You were attacked before leaving, though, and I never heard anything after the initial reports.*"

I had to be careful here.

Lydia might have been on my side most of the time, but she still worked for the Directors. If she had been another human, I could see trusting her, but she was code. Incredibly advanced code, yes, but there was no way to know if she was programmed to edge out her loyalties to me when requests came from my bosses. My guess was they carried more weight than me. That would seem sensible anyway.

The problem was that she'd heard our earlier conversation, so she already knew about the amalgamites.

"*Just some werewolves and mages that we pissed off at one point, I suppose,*" I lied, which seemed to be something I was doing a lot of tonight. "*They caught us by surprise and we had to run. But now that I'm back, I'll be doing a little searching for them. Once the team returns, we'll get the criminals sorted out.*"

"*I thought the crew said they were amalgamites like you, honey tush?*"

"*They did,*" I affirmed, "*but we all know I'm the only one around. Plus, these guys had vampire fangs and were doing magic. My guess is those fangs were fakes.*"

"Hmmm."

She wasn't buying it, which meant I had to use better data points. One thing I'd learned over the years was that if you fed someone bullshit emphatically, they were more likely to believe it, especially if you cited sources that seemed credible. Whether those sources were *actually* credible or not was only a problem if the person you shared the information with was smart enough to fact-check.

Most people weren't smart enough to fact-check.

Too bad Lydia wasn't a 'people.'

Still, if I used my team as those credible sources, she would have to go on historical reference.

In other words, there was a good chance she'd believe me.

"Based on what Griff and Jasmine said," I explained, leaving out Rachel since she wasn't around the other amalgamites when they had attacked, *"the people hitting them were a little too polished."*

"What do you mean?"

"Well, Griff said they were very coordinated, like they were working from a script or something." I quickly added, *"And Jasmine saw one of the guys pushing at his teeth. She thinks maybe he was having trouble with them staying in properly."*

"I see," she said, still not sounding convinced. *"This information came from Griff and Jasmine, you say?"*

"Yep," I answered without hesitation, even though it didn't. *"You know me. I trust my people more than I trust anyone. That includes you, of course."*

"Thank you, sweetums," she replied, sounding chuffed. *"I suppose we must rely on the instincts of our teammates."*

"*Exactly what I was thinking,*" I responded emphatically. "*We are a team, right?*"

"*Most certainly,*" Lydia affirmed in a serious tone.

That was perfect.

I *had* kind of felt bad for leading her astray, and for lying on behalf of my crew, but it was for the greater good. Or at least I assumed it was. Since the Directors hadn't exactly been forthcoming with assistance over the last year, I had no clue what was really going on behind all these ubers…and now amalgamites.

So, for now anyway, Lydia and the Directors had to be kept as much in the dark as possible.

Speaking of which…

"*Are the Directors waiting for me?*" I asked, not really wanting to know. "*I'm assuming you told them of our predicament?*"

"*I report everything to them, pumpkin,*" she replied, possibly giving away more information than necessary. No, Lydia wasn't capable of making mistakes like us. Everything she said or did had data behind it. She may do something wrong, but it was never a mistake. "*They asked to see you the moment you returned.*"

I sighed and looked at the door that sat at the back of my office. The last thing I wanted to do was waste time talking with four dudes who weren't going to help me out of this jam anyway. Plus, I had no idea what I was going to tell them at this point. I doubted leading with, "Hey, guys, guess what? I've got brothers and they appear to be bad guys!" would go over very well.

"*Do they know I'm back?*" I asked Lydia with some hesitation.

"Not yet, lover," she answered. *"I always give you some time before letting them know you've arrived. You seem to appreciate it when I do that."*

"I totally do, you digital deviant."

She giggled mechanically.

"I love that nickname."

"That's only because it's fitting," I said, oiling the gears a little more. "Listen, babe," I added, "would you be willing to not tell them I've arrived yet?"

There was a small delay. *"Why would I do that, honey?"*

"It's just that I don't have anything to tell them right now, and I hate going in there empty-handed."

I glanced down and noted the review forms for my team were sitting in my in-box. I'd have to hook those up soon. After all the help the gang gave me with the valkyries, it'd be a breeze.

"How much time do you need?" she asked, leaving off the flirting.

"A few hours," I responded, surprised she was even considering going along with my request. "I just want to track down the creeps that came after us. Once I find them and get a little information, I'll jump right into that meeting."

"It goes against protocol," she stated, her voice sounding more pedantic by the second. *"I am not supposed to do things against protocol."*

Lydia was a product of her programming, yes, but she was also a lady...sort of. Her core code identified her as such, anyway. While I was no software engineer, I was fantastic at manipulating the fairer sex, digital or otherwise.

"Good thing I like my girls to be feisty and rebellious, then," I said slyly.

"What?"

"One of the main reasons I find you so enticing is that you know when to play by the rules and you know when to rebel," I coaxed her. *"It's a major turn-on to be around a woman with a mind of her own."*

The use of the word 'woman' often made Lydia's chip flutter. I was careful not to overuse it, but sometimes, such as this, it was the perfect word to push her over the edge in the direction I needed her to go.

Another giggle told me it'd worked.

"Do you really think I'm rebellious?"

"Most definitely, baby," I urged, *"and it's sooo hot that you are."*

"Okay, okay," she said, sounding like a school girl who had a crush on the captain of the football team. *"I won't tell them you've arrived yet, but promise me you won't be too long."*

"I'll do my best, you sexy mess of wires," I answered as I bolted out of my office.

CHAPTER 27

My first stop was the weapons room. There were plenty of devices I could use to help protect myself, but I was more interested in setting booby traps at this point. I just didn't know if there'd be anything in here that'd fit the bill.

Empirics were the weapon of choice. They were like little magic grenades that were roughly the size of a thin hockey puck. Beastly things, too.

Unfortunately, they required special authorization to use them.

Yes, I was the chief and so *I* could authorize them without a fuss, but that would bring attention I didn't want at the moment.

That was the rub.

I'd have to enter a special code to open the lock on the box holding those little gems, which would immediately send a signal out to the Directors. I *could* use the skeleton key that Turbo had given me instead of the code. I just didn't know what actually triggered the notification mechanism. If it was the code that opened the lock, Turbo's key would be perfect. But if it was the simple act of opening the door, I'd be caught red-handed.

I couldn't chance it.

That meant Empirics were out.

There were some premade notification runes, which might be useful. They were contained in little orbs that would magically write the rune wherever they were thrown.

I put a couple of those on the table.

The only other options were things like bullets and vests. We almost never wore vests, but we went through bullets like EQK went through curse words.

Bottom line, there just wasn't much I could use here.

Just as I was leaving the room, though, I caught sight of the battle-gear closet. It contained full outfits for each member of the PPD. No, they weren't classy, but they were lightweight, protective, dark, and they fit like a glove.

I opened the door and took out my uniform, making quick work of changing. The only thing I didn't like was wearing the boots. They weren't heavy or anything, but I was just more of a loafers kind of guy.

Once dressed, I checked myself in the mirror.

It was a good look.

I mean, it wasn't like I was wearing a Stuart Hughes Diamond Edition suit by any stretch, and I'm sure it would look ridiculous on someone who had a little too much padding around the middle, but it fit me nicely.

Even better, it would do its job in helping me sneak around.

With that thought, I backed away into one of the dark corners. I could see myself just fine because of my ability to see in dim situations, but anyone else wouldn't even notice I was...

Damn.

If my 'brothers' were genuine amalgamites, they'd be able to see me in the dark as well.

Regardless, this outfit was a solid step up from the casual garb I had going, especially since I was planning to lure my prey out into the desert. I'd need to be able to run, roll, jump, dive, and so on. This suit allowed for that much better than my slacks and button-up shirt ensemble.

Another benefit was that this getup would morph along with me if I ended up having to go full wolf—something I *really* didn't want to have happen.

Best of all, I didn't care if it got dirty, bloody, or goopy.

I headed back out the door after tucking Boomy into a holster, filling my jacket with enough breaker bullets to start a small war. I left the notifications runes on the table, though. The fact was that my magic would allow me to reach out better anyway. I'd just have to focus on it.

That's when I ran into Portman, reminding me that notification magic was more passive than active.

"Dex?" said the big man, giving me the once-over.

Portman was huge, but that went along with being a werebear. He was also one of the kindest people I knew. Rough around the edges, sure, and also gruff, but under that exterior was a heart of gold. Oh, he could be vicious when he needed to be, but in general, Portman was an all around good guy.

"Hey, Portman. What are you doing here?"

"Looking for you and the crew," he replied, crossing his massive arms. "You guys went radio silent for a while there. Just wanted to check in to make sure everything was okay." He gave me another once-over. "You going to a costume party or something?"

"Not exactly."

"Then?"

On the one hand, I didn't want to let him in on my plan anymore than I had wanted to tell my direct team about it; on the other hand, if I *didn't* make it back alive, there needed to be someone who could tell my team what had happened to me.

So with more than a little trepidation, I pushed past him and headed for the exit.

"Follow me and I'll tell you."

CHAPTER 28

We got out to the garage, when I realized I didn't have my Aston Martin with me. I'd left it back at my condo before transporting down to meet my crew at the reintegration center.

There were a couple of marked vehicles I could use, but I hated driving those things. We didn't have the cool sporty models in the PPD. Ours were those blocky-built fuckers that looked like they could have been on the set in Mayberry while Andy Griffith was still filming.

Being seen in one of those could ruin my reputation in this town. It was bad enough I didn't even have a proper suit on.

"All right," I said, once I felt confident we wouldn't be overheard, but then I stopped and gave Portman a look. "Your connector *is* off, right?"

"Is now," he replied.

Good thing I'd asked.

"You have to keep this to yourself," I warned.

He nodded.

"This afternoon Rachel and I were getting it on in the shower—"

He grimaced at me and I stopped speaking.

"Is this the part where I'm supposed to take my pants down and hand you a twenty-dollar bill, Dex?"

"Ew…what?"

"You're starting out your little story like a phone-sex operator," he replied. "I don't want to hear about your sex life. It's bad enough I don't have one of my own."

"I thought you were married."

"Exactly."

"Oh."

"Anyway," he said, "can we move past that part of your story?"

"Right. Well, we were attacked by werewolf assassins."

He tilted his head at me. "You were attacked by people who assassinate werewolves?"

"Huh?" I frowned at him, wondering what the hell he was talking about. Then I replayed my words over in my head and heard it too. "No, I meant they were werewolves who were hired to assassinate me and Rachel." I chewed my lip for a moment. "I mean, I suppose they probably *would* assassinate other werewolves, but…"

I sighed.

"Seeing that you're still alive, I'll leap to the conclusion that they failed," he mused. "Well, that and the fact that I dispatched some people to pick up bodies from your condo. A couple of them were still alive."

"Yep."

"Honestly, hadn't thought much of it because you seem to get attacked at least once a month," he noted.

"True," I agreed. "Anyway, we got a call soon after we wiped out the wolves. Griff and Chuck were attacked, and so were Jasmine, Felicia, Serena, and Warren."

He gave me a look. "Separately?"

"Yeah, Chuck and Griff were attacked at their condo, and the other four were attacked while at Jasmine's place."

"Jasmine, Felicia, Serena, and Warren all live together?" he said with a gasp. "I didn't know that."

"No, they don't. They were, uh…" I trailed off.

Portman was the one who'd said he didn't want to be informed about people's sex lives, so I didn't continue. Personally, I never understood what the big deal was regarding talking about it. I guess some people were more private than others. I'd bet the ones who kept everything behind closed doors were the freakiest of the bunch. Of course, maybe that's why they didn't want to talk about it.

"That part isn't important," I said, pushing forward. "The point is that they were also attacked."

"By assassins who happened to be werewolves?"

"No, by men who appeared to amalgamites."

His eyes went wide at that revelation.

Everyone in the supernatural community knew I was one of a kind…especially the ladies.

Sorry, couldn't resist.

I was internationally famous because of what I was. That fame wasn't necessarily a good thing, either. Most supers despised me because they were all into purity of their kind and such. I found that closed-minded and exceedingly ignorant, but some people had the need to feel superior to others. Funny thing was that people who were that way tended to excel at mediocrity, or worse.

"You heard me right," I stated before Portman could comment. "We don't know if they're genuine or some type of magical concoction meant to lure me into a trap, but that's why I'm wearing the funny cop suit."

"Uh..." His eyebrows fought to connect with each other. "You're wearing the suit because you don't want to be lured into a trap?"

"No," I said slowly. "I'm wearing the suit because I'm planning to face them down and take them out."

"Oh, right. That makes more sense." He finally uncrossed his arms. "Where's the rest of the crew?"

"They're in the Badlands having crazy se..." I paused and glanced up at the big man. "Sorry, I mean they're currently indisposed."

He frowned and shook his head.

"I *knew* I should have been a cop instead of a mortician. You guys have all the damn fun."

"Yeah, right," I scoffed. "If you consider constantly fighting for your life as supers try to shred your flesh 'fun,' Portman, you've got a weird outlook on life."

"At least you're getting laid."

"According to you," I countered, "that's got nothing to do with my being a cop. It's simply a product of my not being married."

He grunted in response to that.

"Anyway," I continued, "I didn't want the crew

involved because if those guys really are amalgamites, it could get bloody."

"Yeah," he agreed. "So what's your plan?"

"Get them to follow me out to the desert," I answered. "I don't want to fight them in town. Too many people could get hurt."

"True."

"But I was hoping to pick up some decent weapons and boobytraps while I was here." I shrugged at him. "I couldn't even chance picking up any of our Empirics."

"Why not?" he asked, looking confused. "They're yours, aren't they?"

I went into the discussion regarding how different the Directors had been acting ever since the ubers had started infecting the Strip. I explained their odd behavior, and also gave him the inside scoop regarding Gabe and all the special abilities he'd given me over the year.

By the time I'd finished, Portman looked like a man who understood exactly why I didn't want to risk my team at this point.

I was relieved at that, because I knew damn well my crew was going to be more than pissed when they figured out what was really going on. I just hoped I'd still be alive when they came to cuss me out.

"Okay, Dex," Portman said after a few moments of thought, "here's what we're gonna do. We'll take the morgue van back to my place. I've got tons of explosives and other goodies. Been stockpiling them in case the supers decide to go batshit crazy at some point. We'll pile some stuff up in my Jeep and head out to the desert, get set up, and wait for your buddies."

I honestly didn't know what to say to that. In fact, I was kind of shocked by his offer. Sure, we were friends, but he would be putting his life on the line here.

"I'm sorry, Portman," I eventually said, "but I can't ask you to do that."

He crossed his arms again.

"You didn't."

CHAPTER 29

Based on the fact that Portman said he was one of those doomsday people who stored up weapons and such, I'd assumed we'd be driving to a trailer park to pick up supplies.

Boy, was I ever wrong.

His place was pretty posh. It was white with a beautiful brown roof and etchings. There wasn't much of a yard in the front, but I was guessing that the back yard extended nicely because the houses on the way in that had the short front yard all had the big back yard.

"*You* live here?" I said, probably sounding quite like a knob.

"Yeah," he said, and then gave me a look. "Why'd you say it like that?"

"Huh? Oh…uh…I just…" I trailed off. "Nothing. Never mind."

I got out of the van and followed him up to the front

door. He fumbled with his keys for a second and then pushed inside.

The place was immaculate.

There were hardwood floors straight through. The walls were painted in earthen tones, with sparsely hung artwork around each room. His furniture was primarily leather, which I kind of expected, but this was stuff you picked up at high-end joints. I didn't know how much they were paying Portman to run the supernatural morgue, but damn.

"I gotta say, man," I stressed, "your house is stunning."

"It's a place to hang my hat," he replied, like it was nothing. "House like any other, I'd say."

"Well, if I ever do a makeover at my place, I'll have to give your wife a call."

He raised an eyebrow and tilted his head down at me. "Two things, Dex: One, she didn't do the design, I did; and two, stay away from my wife."

I started to laugh, but he looked serious.

"Why does everyone think I'm such a cad?" I asked to the air, losing my humor. "I don't screw around with married women, Portman. Besides, you're a friend of mine, so even if I was lacking in morals, I'd hope to still have enough respect for you not to be a homewrecker." I then shook my head at him. "And why would she want me anyway? She's got a burly werebear for a husband. I can't compete with that."

"Yeah, right," he snorted, and then walked out into the garage.

"Especially not one who can decorate like you can," I called after him.

He smacked the button on the wall and the garage door opened up before he started loading things into the Jeep like it was practiced. There were shovels, rope, and a series of weapons. But what worried me were the two big bags of lime.

"Done this before, Portman?" I asked, feeling like I was at the scene of an investigation. "Not many people have all these items sitting in their garage, you know."

"I've done it once or twice," he answered as he continued dumping stuff into the vehicle. "I helped Chief Michaels a couple times before you were on the force in Vegas."

Chief Michaels was the man I had replaced. He was one of my mentors as well. Great guy, but he could be tough and rugged when he wanted to be. And now that I was seeing a new side of Portman, it was clear that my old chief sometimes took matters into his own hands.

"Don't think things like that," The Admiral said flatly. *"You and I are still on shaky ground."*

"Shut up."

"I don't think I want to know the details of those arrangements," I said.

"Good thing," Portman replied with a grunt. He'd just dumped a huge duffel bag into the back seat. "Wasn't planning to tell you anyway."

"Right."

He motioned for me to hop in and get my seatbelt on. Within minutes we were cruising down the road toward the desert.

I didn't know if my 'brothers' knew I was back in town or not, but my assumption was they'd soon figure it out. If

I kept moving, it'd make things trickier on them. At least I hoped so because that was my plan.

Portman and I just needed to get everything set up first.

What that 'everything' was, I didn't know yet, but based on the amount of crap Portman had loaded into the Jeep, I was guessing it'd be interesting.

"You said there were four of them, right?" he asked as the wind blew through my hair.

"Yeah."

"That it?"

Honestly, I hadn't considered that there could be more. Four was bad enough. I hadn't met them yet, no, but if they had the ability to pin down my crew, they were clearly pretty powerful.

"I hope so," I replied.

"Me, too," he laughed. "Can't imagine you fighting four of yourself."

"I've been pretty heavily modified recently," I told him, hoping that his loyalties to the Directors weren't as heavy as Lydia's. I hated sharing information about my new situation with anyone, but if Portman was willing to stand by my side then I owed him the truth. "I'm basically a full mage, werewolf, vampire, werebear, and everything now. All my skills and genetic tidbits hit full when I was bitten by a vampire." I breathed out heavily. "I'm trying to keep that under wraps, though, so please don't tell anyone."

He shot me a look. "Who am I going to tell?"

"The Directors, maybe?"

"Nah, Dex," he said, shaking his head firmly. "I don't trust those bastards. Once a person gets to their position of power, things get dicey. Priorities shift. Maybe it's for the greater good, maybe not. But I don't like dangling from the end of a string." He pressed the accelerator. "Screw them, Dex. Chief of the PPD is about as far as I allow my trust to go."

That was essentially an outright admission that Portman trusted me. I suppose I shouldn't have been surprised at that. I'd never done anything to give him reason to feel otherwise.

"Thanks," I said sincerely. "I appreciate that."

He shrugged.

"One day you'll get promoted," he added with a wink. "Then I won't trust you any more either."

I cracked a smile. "Probably wise."

"Yep."

CHAPTER 30

We headed out toward Mt. Charleston, going off-road so we wouldn't be too near the houses. It was clear that Portman had a plan for our final destination.

"You sure they'll be able to track you?" he asked as we finally pulled to a stop. "No point in doing all this if they ain't gonna show up."

"I don't know for sure," I admitted, "but I've got the feeling they'll find me. If not, I'll make some noise."

Light pollution wasn't horrible out where we were, which meant the sky opened up and the stars made me glad to be alive. Hopefully, I'd stay that way. I used to head out to the desert every now and then just to look up at the stars. It gave me time to think, unwinding from the stress of being a cop.

I didn't get to do that much anymore, now that Rachel and I were back together. She wasn't fond of the outskirts and I wasn't fond of getting grief over leaving her alone while I went stargazing by myself.

"So, you brought a ton of stuff," I announced as he began unloading everything. "I'm assuming that means you have a plan?"

"Yep," he replied. "I've practiced out here a bunch of times over the last few years. Already got a lot of things set up, too, just have to pull the safeguards."

"Safeguards?"

He squinted at me. "Makes it so people don't accidentally—"

"I know what the term 'safeguard' means, Portman," I interrupted him while wearing a grimace. "I'm asking what you've done out here that would require a safeguard?"

"Ah, right," he replied with a grin. Then, he pointed at one of the duffel bags. "Bring that along and I'll show you."

When I first went to lift the bag, I thought I was going to dislocate my shoulder. Whatever the hell he had in there was damn heavy. From the clinking sounds, I assumed metals of some sort.

"What in the world do you have in here, man?" I grunted as I heaved it over my head so that I'd have some balance. "Anvils?"

"Explosives, mostly," he answered over his shoulder.

I immediately slowed my walk as my blood ran cold.

"Explosives?" I yelped. "What the fuck am I carrying explosives around for?"

"Because we're going to blow stuff up, Dex," he called back. "Isn't that why we're out here?"

"Well…yeah, but you could have told me before I just started banging this bag around."

"They're secured," he laughed. "It'd take a lot more than just knocking them against each other for you to activate what I've got in there."

He put his hand out to stop me. He was studying the area carefully. Obviously, we were near his playground.

"Bush," he said, pointing. "Large rock, small rock, and flat stone."

He paused but kept scanning.

Being that I was a dick, I started pointing at things and naming them too.

"Cactus, dirt, pebbles…"

I trailed off as he turned around, giving me a sinister look.

"You *do* realize I can punch a hole through your chest, right?" he asked without inflection.

"Not in my current state, my friend," I countered. "You wouldn't last five seconds."

"Is that a challenge?"

"No," I answered, forgetting that Portman wasn't one to take challenges lightly, even if they were intended as simple ribbing. "Just riling myself up for my upcoming battle."

"*Our* upcoming battle," he corrected me.

"Yeah," I said, wanting to tell him he wasn't going to be around for the actual fight, but I needed him to help me set up first. That meant he had to keep thinking he'd be part of the mayhem. "Anyway, you were going to show me something with safeguards and all that?"

He nodded and told me to stay put.

Then, he carefully walked around the area, touching each of the items he had named before. Bush, large rock, small rock, and flat stone. I couldn't see what he was doing to them, precisely, but after he'd completed messing with the last item, they all began to glow slightly.

A few seconds later, the ground shifted and the glowing faded.

I looked down, taking a step backward.

Unless my eyes were deceiving me, which was doubtful considering my impeccable night vision, there was a massive platform, and it had a large, flat bar connected to it that ran straight out to a wheel of some sort. All of it was nearly flush with the ground, and since every piece was flat, except for the wheel that was masked by a few rocks near it, a person walking on any piece of the thing would just think they had stepped into a very slight shallow section of the ground.

"Is that what I think it is?" I asked, not believing my eyes.

"That depends," Portman replied. "If you think it's a catapult, then yep."

Why would he need a catapult out here? It wasn't exactly an efficient weapon, after all, unless it fired really fast, at varying distances, and could rotate in order to strike all angles. But even if that had been the case, wouldn't a gun be more effective in keeping people at bay?

"I'm assuming you can adjust it?" I asked, baffled.

"Some," he affirmed, "but it ain't for firing *at* people, Dex."

"Oh, okay then." I nodded as I continued staring at it.

"Actually, no, that's not okay. What the hell is it for, if not to fire on people?"

He smiled like a hyena who was about to have lunch.

"Launching them."

"Huh?"

He walked over and picked up a medium-size rock like it was nothing. I'd have guessed the one he'd selected was at least eighty pounds. Clearly, Portman was a very strong man.

"It's a pressure-sensitive switch. Anything over fifty pounds steps on it and zing!"

"Zing?"

"Watch," he said, stepping over and dropping the rock on the platform from behind.

A split second later, that rock was airborne, and it was quite a liftoff. It went a good one hundred feet into the air, fast. Based on the arc and the resulting thud of the landing, I'd also wager it landed a good quarter of a mile out.

"Holy fuck bubbles, Portman," I laughed. "Where the hell'd you get that idea?"

"I come up with all sorts of things," he answered. "The odder, the better. One person flying off due to this thing is going to make everyone else walk a hell of a lot slower, which will give me time to pick them off one by one."

After a hearty chuckle, he walked back over to the flat rock and pressed a few buttons, resetting the catapult to its resting position. Another few taps and something really cool happened.

The ground covered over.

It was clearly an illusion, but it was seamless. If you

didn't know any better, you'd have thought you were just walking over a small patch of land. The deception would make the shallow feeling of stepping onto any part of the contraption even less suspicious.

It'd probably take your brain at least a second to figure out that your wrong step had just morphed you into a projectile.

Not fun.

"I honestly never knew you were this warped, Portman," I said, feeling both impressed and concerned. Ultimately, though, being impressed won out. "I gotta say, I think I like it."

"Good thing," he remarked, "'cause there's also a tarpit, a spike pit, and a magical flame thrower." He leaned in. "I had to get some help from Warren to hook that last one up."

That admission jolted me. Why would Warren be out here helping with something like this? He didn't strike me as someone who would be into doomsday junk.

"Warren?"

"Yep. Weird guy, but he knows his stuff." Portman motioned again to the ground where the catapult was hidden. "Covering up the catapult with a thin film of reality was his idea, too."

"No way."

"Yep."

"Anyone else on my team work on this stuff with you?"

"Griff consulted early on," he said, motioning for me to follow him, "but he stopped a few years back when he and Chuck took things to the next level in their relationship."

We spent the next thirty minutes going over the tarpit, the spike pit, and the flame thrower. All of these things were going to be used when I faced my 'brothers.' Whether any of them would work against them or not was yet to be seen, but my only hope was that they'd prove to make enough of a distraction to allow me to attack.

After we layered the area with the explosives, Portman turned to me and rubbed his hands together.

"This should be fun," he said, grinning from ear to ear. His hair was standing on end. "I'm ready to fight."

"Yeah," I said, clearing my throat. "About that…uh, I'm going to need you to leave the area."

He chuckled. "Good one, Dex."

I let out a slow breath, knowing that I'd probably have to force the situation here. I didn't want to have to do that, but I would if necessary. There was just no way I was going to risk Portman's life any more than I would have risked any member of my direct team.

"I'm not joking," I said seriously.

His smile faded.

"You're being serious?" he rasped.

"Yes."

"Well…tough shit," he scoffed at me, his face growing dark. "I don't leave my friends to fight on their own, Dex, even if they're currently being assholes."

Apparently, I was going to have to step it up.

Recalling what happened when I compelled Rachel earlier, I stood my ground and allowed magic to flow into my voice.

"You will follow my orders, Portman," I stated firmly,

feeling the power flow through my voice. "You *will* clear the area."

For the first time since I'd met Portman, I saw something in his face I'd never thought possible.

Fear.

It was intoxicating.

CHAPTER 31

*P*ortman stood there staring at me for another few seconds. It was clear that he was going through some inner turmoil. His caveman brain probably wanted to reach out and snap me in two, but my magic was holding him in place.

I cleared my throat and he jolted for a moment. Then, he shook his head and blinked a few times.

"What happened?" he said, looking unsure.

"What do you mean?" I replied, pretending everything was normal.

"I..." He furrowed his brow and then glanced away. "Weird. Anyway, what are we doing again?"

Obviously, not everyone responded the same way to being compelled. Rachel and Portman had both looked somewhat frightened, but Rachel hadn't drifted off into a fog, only returning to wonder what had just occurred.

"You were going to hop in your Jeep and drive to a spot where you could see the goings on down here," I explained. The truth was that we had never agreed to anything, but I was hoping he didn't know that. "If all goes well, you'll come back and pick me up and we'll head off to the station; if not, you'll blow up the entire area and head back to the station to let everyone know what happened here."

He grunted out a "huh" sound.

"I don't remember any of that," he fretted.

"You could stay here and fight, if you'd prefer?" I asked, hoping that my magic from before would trigger and he'd have no part of that concept. "Up to you."

"No, no," he replied, his face going white. "I...no."

"Okay, then." I slapped him on the arm. "So, what *are* you going to do, exactly?"

He ran his fingers through his hair as his face contorted. It was abundantly clear that his mind was in a serious state of flux at the moment.

Part of me wanted to be proud of that fact because it demonstrated how much power I truly had flowing through my veins.

My mages were right, though.

If I succumbed to this power, I would become a monster.

"I'm going to drive up one of the hills," Portman said after a few moments. "If I see you win, I'm going to blow up the area."

"No," I corrected him. "You're *not* going to blow up the area if *I* win, Portman."

"Oh, right," he hissed. "Sorry. If you start to lose, I'll blow up the area."

"Wrong again," I stated flatly. "If I am *killed*, you'll blow up the area so the other amalgamites die with me."

"Ah yeah, that's it," he said, pointing at me offhandedly. "Everything is kind of fuzzy right now for some reason."

Indeed, it was, and it would remain that way so I could be sure that Portman would survive this night, regardless of what happened to me. The power part of my current persona disagreed with that sentiment, pushing my thoughts instead toward using the massive werebear of a man as fodder in the upcoming battle.

Um…no.

"If you win," he continued, "I'll drive back to the precinct and let everyone know."

"*We'll* drive back to the precinct," I amended for him.

He frowned again. "But you'll be there, right?"

"Not if I win, Portman," I said as if he were missing a few marbles. To be fair, he was. "Why would I want to be stranded in the middle of the desert while you're back at the precinct?"

"Oh, yeah," he said. "I guess that makes sense. But, wait—"

"Listen carefully," I commanded, using the voice again, "you're going to drive up to a hill where you can watch the fight. If I win, you will come back down here and pick me up; if I lose, you will detonate the explosives and then return to the precinct and await my crew, telling them everything that's happened." I had an edge in my voice that felt capable of cutting through steel. "Are we clear?"

"Yes," he whispered like a man who had just seen a ghost.

"Good."

The rush of power was delectable, but I had to resist it. I did *not* want to turn into the very ubers I'd been fighting over the past year. They were douchebags, and I didn't want to be a douchebag.

I suddenly felt a shift in the air. Not a physical shift, per se, but just…something was off.

Familiar, yet wrong at the same time.

I reached out with my new powers just as a set of car lights came into view out in the distance.

My 'brothers' had arrived.

CHAPTER 32

I shuffled Portman off to his Jeep, giving him a little extra magical encouragement. Honestly, that was a damn good power to have, even if it was tickling my desire to rule the universe. Something told me that temptation was only going to worsen as I faced the oncoming amalgamites.

Two minutes after Portman disappeared around a corner, the lights on the incoming car turned off as it stopped about a football field's distance away.

The doors opened and closed.

I stared out at my 'brothers.'

If I were to run into them on the street, I wouldn't have considered them related to me by any stretch of the imagination. It was only because they had shown the ability to cast spells and produce fangs that made them suspicious. Well, that and the fact that they attacked my team while wearing nice clothes.

I had to admit that their outfits *were* nice.

Another indicator that we were possibly related was that they still wore those suits even while out in the desert looking for a fight. I was notorious for doing that.

They approached, staying just on the opposite side of Portman's playground.

I didn't know if they were able to spot his toys or if they were just being cautious because of me. I'd hoped for the latter considering *I* was unable to spot Portman's toys. If they could see them, that would mean they were more advanced than I was, even in my current state.

That'd be bad.

Each face was different, meaning that they weren't exact duplicates of me. My team *had* said that they weren't doppelgängers, so I should have known that, but I just wasn't sure what to expect.

They all had dark hair, chiseled jawlines, and nice suits. That's where our similarities ended, though, at least in the realm of looks and fashion.

But there was something else about them that seemed…off.

It was like they were unfinished.

I know it sounded odd, but imagine a mannequin coming to life while retaining their exact look. It was like that with these guys. Not a wrinkle in the bunch. In fact, it was almost as if they were androids or something.

That made my blood freeze.

Were my 'brothers' actually androids?

I frowned at myself, pictured Rachel calling me an 'idiot,' and then refocused on reality.

"What's up, guys?" I asked, giving them a small wave.

"You will come with us," they replied as one.

No delay either. I'm talking a full-on chorus of voices saying the exact same thing at the exact same time.

"Damn," I remarked. "Did you guys practice that or something?"

"You will come with us," they repeated.

That time they all pointed at me simultaneously. There was one anomaly, though. While three of them used their right hands to point, the second one from the right used his left.

The rest of them glared at him accusingly.

He lowered his left arm and lifted his right.

The others sighed in unison and turned back to me.

Their looks of disdain *definitely* reminded me of…well, me.

"Where are we going exactly?" I asked.

"You will come with us," was their only response.

"Not unless you answer some questions first," I replied, crossing my arms in defiance. "Like, for example, are you guys Borg or something?"

They started with their, "You will…", but they paused and said, "Huh?"

"You know what I'm talking about," I answered. "Those dudes in *Star Trek* who are part of the collective."

"We are amalgamites," they chorused.

"That's really creepy," I grunted with a shudder. "I mean, I'm glad you said 'amalgamites' instead of 'amalgamite.' Otherwise, I'd have thought you were definitely part of a hive mind."

They didn't reply, but they *did* all squint at me at the same time.

"Right," I continued, "so it's clear that you're not exactly smart."

"I am," said the guy who'd raised his left hand during the pointing fiasco earlier.

"Quiet, Kevin," the rest of them warned.

Kevin was the one who went against the grain. That was good. If I played it right, maybe I could turn that to my advantage. With any luck, I might even be able to get him on my side.

It was a reach, but it was also definitely worth a shot.

"Kevin," I said quickly, "you seem different than the rest of these guys."

"We are all different," he replied.

"Yeah, right, but I mean you appear to be the kind of guy who thinks for himself." I wagged a finger at him. "I'd go as far as to say that you should be the leader of this band of four you've got here."

"Bertram is the leader," Kevin replied, pointing to the guy at the end.

"Is that right, Bertram?"

"You will come with us," Bertram replied in perfect timing with the others, except for Kevin. He was a little behind them this time. Bertram dropped his chin to his chest with a groan. Then he turned to his brother. "Honestly, Kevin, you need to get with the program."

"Sorry," Kevin replied, looking sheepish. "I don't care about the formalities, Bertram. You know I'm only here because I love to kill, maim, and torture."

"Hopefully not in that order," I said with a chuckle.

"What's wrong with the order I listed those items?" Kevin asked, clearly confused.

I found that I was shaking my head along with the other three amalgamites.

So much for Kevin being the smart one.

"Forget it," I said. "So you *like* hurting and killing?"

"No," he replied in a serious tone. "I *love* hurting and killing. It's the only thing that brings me joy in life."

I jolted at that. "Well, you're a sick fucker, then, aren't you?"

"Yes," he hissed with a smile that a demon would envy. I hadn't expected him to take that as a compliment. "The screams bring me pleasure."

My eyebrows shot up at that admission.

"Oookay." I studied the rest of the amalgamites. "Are the rest of you equally batshit crazy or is it just Kevin?"

"It's just Kevin," all four of them replied.

Yes, *all* four of them. Kevin spoke of himself in the third-person that time.

I was still thinking it might be a good move to get Kevin on my side, even if he was nuts. I just needed to convince him that killing his brothers would be the ultimate in fun. If that didn't work, maybe I could turn them against Kevin. Getting them to kill each other was better than me having to fight all four of them at once.

But right now I wanted to get some more answers. These were the only people in the world who were like me. That meant they had access to information I could never find on my own.

"How old are you all?"

"We are forty-one," three of them answered.

"Thirty-nine," came the final response.

Again, Kevin was the outlier.

I just want to point out that the admission of their ages was another indication that these guys were too perfect. If you were to look at them on the street, you would have assumed they weren't a day over twenty-one. They were *that* flawless.

"Do you all have the last name 'Dex,' too?"

"Yes."

Another tick in the 'Yep, we're actually brothers' column.

"Where are your parents?" I asked.

"Irrelevant question," they replied, including Kevin.

"It's not irrelevant to me," I argued.

"Don't care," they countered as one.

I chewed my lip for a moment.

"Did you all grow up together?"

"Yes."

"Did your father teach you how to play catch?" I asked, trying to be tricky.

"Irrelevant question," said three of them.

"Yes," said Kevin. Then, "Sorry."

"So that means you *did* have a father."

They all stared at Kevin. He looked at his fingernails.

"It must have been nice having a family," I sighed. "Do you guys get together for holidays and such?"

"Irrelevant question," said three of them, and then they quickly added, "Quiet, Kevin."

He just rolled his eyes.

Translation: They *did* get together for holidays.

"Yeah, yeah, I get it," I said after a moment. "You don't want to share with me because you guys are just a basket of dicks."

Kevin nodded his agreement.

The implication of his nod suggested that it may be better for me to get him on my side to fight his brothers. Yes, he'd be difficult to defeat one on one, but it'd still be easier than if I were to fight him *and* the other three at the same time.

The problem was how to get him to my side?

"Kevin," I said, rubbing my hands together, "how would you like to kill, maim, and torture your shitty brothers?"

"What?" everyone but Kevin chorused.

His face fell.

"I'm not allowed to do that," he sulked, "but I sure would love to."

"Idiot," said the brothers, this time not quite in unison.

"Are you going to let them talk to you like that, Kevin?" I pressed. "They've done nothing but push you around since you got here, and do you know why?"

He shook his head at me.

"I'll tell you why, Kevin," I said as someone who was an authority on the topic. "It's because they're all jealous and afraid of you. They know you're better than them. You're smarter, younger, stronger, and you're willing to kill, maim, and torture in any order that you damn well please."

The area went completely silent for a moment.

Everyone was clearly weighing my words. The three brothers looked more than worried and Kevin appeared conflicted.

Perfect.

"You will do as you are told, Kevin," Bertram stated,

speaking on his own this time. "If you do not, I will kill you myself."

That was the wrong thing to say.

You see, there are just some people that you don't say stuff like that to. They don't respond well to it. Take Portman, for example. If I hadn't used compelling magic on him when I told him to scoot along, I'd be eating my meals from a straw for a month. It was just the nature of things.

"Do *not* speak to me like that," Kevin growled at his brother, which made Bertram take a concerned step backward. "*Never* speak to me like that."

"Did you see that, Kevin?" I jumped in quickly. "Bertram is afraid. His fear is so strong it's almost glowing. You like…" I paused. "No, you *love* seeing that, don't you?"

"Yes," Kevin replied, his eyes glistening in the moonlight. "I *do* love it."

"Stop," the other two brothers warned Kevin. "We will be forced to destroy you if you attack Bertram."

Kevin's venomous face changed so fast to one of pure terror that I'd be surprised if he hadn't pulled a muscle. He backed down, turning forward again while swallowing hard.

"I apologize, Bertram," Kevin breathed. "Our brother tricked me."

Was *I* the 'brother' in that comment? I had to be, right?

Shit.

These warped fuckers were indeed my family.

Too bad I was going to have to kill them.

Before the fun could begin, though, I had one more question.

"Do we have any other brothers?" I asked.

"No."

"Sisters?"

"One."

I had a sister! Cool!

"What's her name?"

"Wynn."

"Wynn Dex?" I laughed. "Does she do windows?"

"What?" they asked.

"Forget it." I was going through a mix of emotions at the moment. "Where is she?"

"Irrelevant question."

CHAPTER 33

I was standing at a crossroad and genuinely had no idea how to proceed.

On the one hand, these guys were my family. Unfinished, sure, and more than a bit odd...especially Kevin. But didn't all families have that one freak who stood out among the rest? And if you think your family *doesn't* have one of those freaks, it's *you*.

Conversely, it was abundantly clear that my brothers —note that I'm not using the air quotes anymore because it'd become pretty damn clear that we were related—were *not* good people.

That, in turn, suggested that our father hadn't been such a great guy either.

He'd named his daughter Wynn Dex, after all.

Oh, shit, could that mean my father was the owner of the Wynn? It would explain why I had been given all this money. It would also explain my fashion sense. But I didn't look anything like the guy, and neither did my brothers. It would also mean my father was still alive!

"One more thing," I said anxiously, holding up a finger, "our father isn't Steve Wynn, right?"

"No!"

Their response was given in such a way that you'd have thought I'd insulted them. Or maybe they were covering up?

"Kevin?" I pushed.

"He's not our father," Kevin replied, even though his brothers seemed displeased by him speaking alone. Obviously, Kevin was feeling somewhat empowered at the moment. "My brothers and I have answered honestly."

"Is he still alive, at least?" I pleaded.

They went back to their old standard.

"You will come with us."

Damn it.

While it was becoming more and more clear that my father wasn't a nice person, I'd at least hoped to have met the guy. As it stood, I had a feeling that wasn't going to be an option.

"All right, then," I declared, "if you want me to join you, I'll comply, but only on one condition."

"What is your condition?" they asked.

"That Kevin be allowed to come over here and shake my hand."

They all looked at each other in confusion.

"Why?"

"Because that's my rule," I replied firmly. I then waved at Kevin. "Come on over."

He looked unsure, but his brothers shrugged at him, so he began walking.

I had been careful to stand in the perfect spot for what happened next.

Kevin stepped on the platform that was hidden under the magical covering, signaling that they could *not* see Portman's toys. An almost imperceptible click sounded a split second later, and Kevin flew off into the night while yelling in horror.

That was going to leave a mark.

The other brothers watched him fly away, giving me the opportunity to take off toward the next bit of fun.

CHAPTER 34

By the time I got to the tarpit, the brothers were hot on my tail. They were launching energy balls at me, but I had a shield in place to deflect them. Besides, I had a feeling that they weren't looking to kill me anyway. At least not yet. They were adamant that I join them, and they never specified that with an ultimatum.

I scrambled past the pit and tapped a code into the rock on the other side, just as Portman had taught me. There was a gentle hiss and then a slight shimmering, signaling that the ground cover had slid away and the magical facade now camouflaged the deadly trap that lay beneath.

The first brother to the scene went face first into the pit, causing the illusion to disappear.

The other two backed off, staring down.

I lit up a couple of fireballs in my hand and looked at the pit.

"I'd hate to have to kill him," I pointed out, "but unless you tell me where we're going, I *will* do it."

"You have already killed Kevin," Bertram stated, speaking on his own. "For this, we thank you. However, we will not be pleased if you kill Leo."

"I don't want to kill, uh, Leo either," I admitted, and it was true. This *was* my family, for goodness sake. "But I have a feeling that you guys are not good people, and if your intention is to turn me into a bad guy...well, no."

"The world will submit to us or they will die," the three brothers roared like wild beasts, though Leo was clearly struggling. "They need our might and our power, and we will rule with an iron fist, crushing any who dare stand in our way. Order will break through and chaos will fade. We will become the law. Blood will flood the streets. Souls will cry in pain. Death will take both young and old, male and female...and transgenders, too."

I just stood there blinking when they'd finished. My mouth was hanging open.

They will become the law? Did that mean the Directors were behind them...us? What the fuck?

"Nice speech," I rasped. "I especially enjoyed how you added the transgender bit at the end of it."

"We are not prejudiced," Bertram explained. "We shall kill any and all who stand in the way of order and justice, and we shall do so with fairness and equality."

"Right, I got that."

Okay, so that pretty much stuck a nail in the coffin of my having a family. Blood relatives or not, I wasn't like these guys, and I had no intention of becoming like them either...even if my current magical capabilities pleaded for me to be.

And I was damn sure going to be having words with the Directors about this shit as it was becoming clearer by the second why they'd been so close-lipped with me over the last year.

They *wanted* this to happen!

At least that was my running hypothesis, which was admittedly based on some loose suppositions at the moment.

Regardless, if it *was* them, then they clearly hadn't counted on me being who I was.

Or maybe they had?

Fuck!

"I don't suppose I can change your minds on this?" I asked hopefully. "I *really* don't want to have to kill you guys."

"Agony and death come to all who oppose us," they chimed, "including you."

"I had a feeling you'd say something like that," I groaned with a sad shrug. "Ah well, I guess this has to happen, then."

I launched a fireball at the pit. It shot up in flames as Leo screamed his last. Amalgamite or not, burning to death in a tarpit was not something your super healing was going to fix.

That left only Betram and...

Actually, I didn't know the other guy's name.

"Hey," I said as the eyes on my two final brothers smoldered, "what's your name?"

He looked over at Bertram and then back at me.

"It no longer matters," he said, growling. "You must die now."

"Either tell me or I'll call you 'Span,'" I warned him.

"Span?"

"Yeah, Span Dex," I said, proud of my own little joke. "Get it?"

"No."

Well, that ruined all the fun.

"Come on, fuckers," I taunted them. "I've got more fun waiting for you."

I ran for the next obstacle.

CHAPTER 35

This time, when I spun around, I found that Bertram and Span were not directly behind me.

"Guys?" I called out, scanning the area. "Hello?"

"Hello," they said from my left.

I jumped and turned toward them.

Their hands were already glowing, and this time they weren't building up energy pulses. Bertram's hands were red and Span's were blue, signaling they were going to go for a fire and ice attack.

My shield would withstand it, but I needed to fire back…unless…

"All right, all right," I said, putting up my hands in surrender. "I give up already."

They eyed me suspiciously. I couldn't say I blamed them for that, seeing as how I'd fooled them multiple times already. But I had to keep playing the game.

The thing was that Span stood only a few feet away

from Portman's spikes. It was a nasty contraption whereby a pole was covered with long, pointy metal sticks. It was wound up via a spring release, similar to that of the catapult. If I could just get him to step on the trigger, he'd be unable to drink a beer without springing a leak.

But how could I get him over there? I couldn't just ask. Then again, I *did* have another skill.

"Hey, Span," I said, using my compelling voice, "scoot over to your right a few steps, would ya?"

He did as I instructed, but Bertram yelled "No!" and dived at him.

It was too late.

The click sounded, the magical illusion disappeared, and a massive pole unhinged, sweeping directly at my brothers. The grotesque sound of flesh being stabbed made me wince. I also triggered the magical flamethrower. Unfortunately it was pointing the wrong way, so it didn't really do much except light up the night for a few seconds.

I walked over to them, seeing the light slowly fading from their eyes.

They looked up at me in unison and said, "Dick."

Death settled in.

Just as I thought everything was said and done, a slow, methodical clapping sounded behind me.

I spun around to find Kevin was standing there. He was covered in dust and his jacket was sufficiently torn.

But he didn't look angry.

If anything, I'd say he appeared relieved.

"I wanted to kill you for flinging me across the desert,"

Kevin said smoothly. Then, he shrugged. "Honestly, I wanted to kill you anyway. It's what I do. But now that you've taken out my brothers, I feel that I need to thank you first."

"First?" I asked, stepping away and getting myself ready. "What do you mean?"

"Oh, I still *have* to kill you," he explained. "It wouldn't do to let you live after what you did to me, but I sincerely want to thank you for destroying my brothers." His face was one of pure elation. "I've been wanting them dead for years. They're such sticklers for protocol. I'm not like them."

"No," I agreed. "You're really not."

His serenity put me on edge. I didn't want to know what the hell went on behind those eyes, but I couldn't imagine it was pleasant. Well, maybe pleasant to *him*, but most anyone else would feel pretty fucking disturbed.

I glanced around the area. There was only one of Portman's contraptions left, and it was to Kevin's right.

"Ah," he said with a slight chuckle as he followed my eyes. "You have another plaything for me to fall for, yes?"

Damn it.

"Uh…"

He reached over and ran his fingers across the rock, and the illusion disappeared, revealing the spike pit.

"How'd you…" I started but stopped when Kevin stepped aside and motioned toward a body that was seated on the ground about fifty feet away.

It was Portman.

"What the hell?"

Kevin stared at me.

"He told me everything," he said. "That's the kind of thing that compelling magic can do, no?"

I swallowed hard. "Is he dead?"

"Not yet," Kevin answered, as if it really didn't matter one way or the other. "I needed him to bring me back here first, and also to teach me how to disable his contraptions." I must have twitched, because he added, "Oh yes, he was very forthcoming with information after I began unraveling his thoughts. I know where his wife lives, you see?" He looked so serene. "Oh, the things a man will do to protect his family."

"You're seriously one sick piece of shit," I seethed.

He grinned in response.

So he had somehow made it to the Jeep, took care of Portman, dug into the werebear's brain to extract needed information, and then got a ride back down. But I should have heard the truck, right?

Speaking of the truck…

"Where's the Jeep?" I asked.

"On the other side of the hill there," Kevin said, pointing. "We couldn't get too close or you'd hear us."

"Ah."

I suppose I should have *felt* their arrival, too, but I'd been so caught up in dealing with the other amalgamites that I clearly missed it.

Kevin clapped his hands three times and Portman got to his feet. He came walking over at a brisk pace.

When he arrived, I studied his eyes, finding them dulled. He was one hundred percent under Kevin's control.

"Now," Kevin said in a jolly tone of voice, "we can go

about this any number of ways, but the ones I find most compelling are either you fighting him, you fighting me, or you fighting us both." He grinned. "Which do you think makes the most sense?"

"Me fighting you, of course," I answered, playing on the fact that Kevin had demonstrated he loved to kill. "If I fight Portman, that will be five seconds at most. He's no match for either you or me, as you already know. But on the off chance that he gets lucky and kills me, then you'll be robbed of the pleasure." I shrugged at him. "Same holds true for my fighting both of you."

"Hmmm."

I put my hands behind my back and began building up energy.

"Now, if you don't mind my being killed by hands other than your own," I added, and then gave him a look, "or if you're too afraid to fight me one on one, then choose as you see fit."

He clearly did not appreciate the implication that he feared fighting me alone. Being ganged up on was a fear he *did* have, which became apparent when Bertram, Leo, and Span had threatened him, but I didn't think Kevin believed I was any match for him. To be fair, I didn't know if I was or not, either.

Now that Portman was in the picture, though, I was going to have to play this carefully.

"Wait a sec," I said, as a thought struck me. "How'd you track down the Jeep anyway?"

"Oh, that," Kevin answered, waving a hand at me. "I landed on the hill up there," he said, pointing. "It hurt rather badly, and I was pretty pissed off, but my body began to heal and about a minute later, this guy came driving up. That allowed me to calm down and plan my next move."

Unreal.

Portman had parked over where the catapult flung stuff. I could only hope he'd done that on purpose, thinking he could finish whoever got flung up there. Obviously, he'd arrived a bit too late.

"Interesting," I said an instant before bringing my hands out from behind my back.

Kevin dived off to the side as I cast a volley of liquid flame at him. It struck the boulder he'd been standing in front of, causing it to sizzle.

My shield buckled a moment later when Kevin flung a seriously powerful mass of energy my way.

I didn't know if our other brothers had the same level of power or not, nor would I ever know seeing as how they were all dead, but this guy was definitely an uber.

"Portman," I commanded with pure magic, "run away now!"

"Portman," countered Kevin, "sit now!"

Portman dropped to a seated position, but he was busily trying to hop away from the scene, using his buttocks. It seemed he had listened to both our commands.

Kevin grinned and fired an energy pulse toward Portman. I cast a shield on my friend at the same time. Part of the energy made it through, causing Portman to grunt and fall over.

"That's the problem with you goody-goody types,"

Kevin cackled. "You'll risk yourselves to save others. It's why you always lose."

I scoffed at him.

"Have you *ever* read a book or seen a movie, pal?" I asked. "The bad guy *rarely* wins."

"True," he sighed, "but you have to admit that it's so much more fun when they do."

I wanted to argue, but he was kind of right. And why did the bad guys get all the cool-looking gadgets? The good guys always inherited the junk that was just slapped together, barely staying intact, and always breaking down. But somehow they won anyway.

There was another thing with bad guys...they always wanted to be even badder.

"You know what, Kevin," I said, lowering my hands "maybe we're going about this all wrong." I put on a serious face. "I was only fighting you because all of you guys were ganging up on me. You know how that is."

He nodded.

"The truth is that I'll bet that you and I could team up and wipe the shit out of anything."

"Why would I need you to do that?" he countered. "I'm strong enough on my own."

"Of course you are," I agreed, egging him on, "but doesn't every evil villain need a sidekick?"

He raised an eyebrow. "Sidekick?"

"Exactly," I replied. "Someone who hangs on your every word, who backs you up in big fights, and who gets you coffee whenever you need it."

He lowered his hands for a moment too.

"I *could* use a coffee right about now," he remarked.

"And what better person to be your sidekick than your little brother?"

"Who?"

I squinted at him. "Me, Kevin. I'm your little brother, remember?"

"Oh, right. Yeah. Sorry." He rubbed his chin. "But I thought you said you didn't want to be a bad guy?"

"I did say that, yes," I admitted, pretending to agree that it was indeed a quandary. Then, I snapped my fingers. "I've got it!"

"What?"

"We have to test my loyalty to you, Kevin."

He weighed that for a moment.

"How?"

"Yes, how?" I agreed, though I knew exactly what I had planned. I allowed a smile to creep upon my face. "Have me walk on over there and kill Portman."

Kevin looked at Portman and then back at me.

"But he's your friend, right?"

"Exactly," I said. "If I can't kill my friend for you, I certainly *won't* kill anyone else for you."

My brother nodded slowly. He *was* crafty, obviously, but I had the feeling he wasn't quite able to grasp the bigger picture, and what I was planning was definitely bigger-picture stuff.

"But I wanted to kill him," he mumbled.

"Okay, then just have me rough him up some."

Kevin's eyes lit up. "You mean like torture?"

"Yes! Yes, that's *precisely* what I mean, Kevin." I began rubbing my hands together. "And if I do that *before* you kill him, you'll get to hear his screams even more."

"Oooh! Hadn't thought of that." His smile was so large that the whites of his teeth were competing against the glow of the moon. "Yes, yes, do that!"

He was clapping his hands like an excited five-year-old who was just told he was going to the Super Bowl.

I gave Kevin a wink and then strode purposefully toward Portman. Just as I got near the rock that controlled the spike pit, I feigned a trip and keyed in the activation sequence. It started a counter from five seconds.

"Damn rocks," I said, pushing myself up and wiping off my PPD suit.

"Yeah," agreed Kevin, "I really hate—"

The ground shimmered and Kevin glanced over, looking confused.

In a smooth motion, I whipped out Boomy and plugged my older brother right on the shoulder, flinging him off balance and sending him careening into the pit.

He yelled out as he fell and then shrieked upon impact.

I rushed over and found him with a spike through his leg and another through his upper-right chest. He was a mess, but he was also still alive.

Thinking quickly, I hopped down into the pit in an empty location and moved over toward Kevin. There wasn't much time before his lights went out forever, so I had to get to him fast.

I reached out and put my hand on his head, hoping that one of the special skills Gabe the vampire had given me would work. It was called *Flashes*, and its job was to tell me something about a person's past so I could plan.

My desire was for it to tell me about my youth, our parents, my sister, and anything else I could get from it.

Nothing happened.

On the hope that I could summon it by using the power directly, I closed my eyes and thought the word with intent.

Flashes.

CHAPTER 36

I was in that familiar room again. It was the one with the large containers that I couldn't help but feel held bodies.

The place looked like a lab of some sort. Whoever's eyes I was looking through for this *Flashes* event was wearing a white robe, so I was guessing scientist or doctor, or both.

I couldn't tell, but I had the distinct impression these were the same eyes I'd looked through during all of the *Flashes* I'd enjoyed. Trust me when I say I use the term 'enjoyed' rather loosely.

The guy got up and started walking down a hallway, glancing left and right at the different enormous canisters. There were no outside windows wherever this place was housed. If I were to guess, I'd have gone with it being underground.

It just seemed so dreary.

We pushed through a doorway that led to a downward-sloping floor. The hallway grew darker and darker until only the dim lighting from the embedded bulbs in the ceiling lit the way. I couldn't feel the temperature, but something told me it was getting colder, too.

Finally, we reached another set of doors. The guy keyed in a code, but I couldn't see that for some reason. His fingers had blurred during those few moments.

When he pushed into the room, I spotted four metallic tables lined up side by side. On each of them were bodies that connected to familiar faces.

My brothers.

Bertram, Leo, Span, and Kevin were lying there, face up, all naked except for a towel that had been laid across their midsections. Their eyes were closed and I couldn't detect any movement to indicate they were breathing. But I didn't sense they were lifeless, either.

The doctor slipped on gloves and then proceeded to poke and prod each of them in turn.

I wanted to look away, but it wasn't really possible since I had no control over *Flashes*.

Fortunately, he didn't do any prostate checks.

That would have been scarring.

Finally, he gave each of them a shot that contained a bluish liquid.

Each set of eyes fluttered for a moment after receiving the injection.

The doctor took off his gloves and threw them into a wastebasket. I watched as he turned on the water in a large, silver sink and began scrubbing his hands. After a good thirty seconds of washing, he rinsed off the soap, dried his hands off on a towel, and then looked up into the mirror.

I felt my stomach sink.

That was a face I'd seen many times over the past year. It was a face I'd grown to hate, but also one I'd learned to trust. Not implicitly, mind you, but the trust *had* been built up, for sure.

But now I was left questioning everything I wanted to believe.

It just didn't make sense.

The face I was staring at belonged to Gabe, and he was smiling.

"Well done, Ian," he said, using my first name. "You have passed all the tests I've set before you over this year. I am impressed and quite proud."

What the fuck was going on?

"Disposing of your brothers was the final obstacle," he added. "Now, you must come and see me."

He turned away.

"Where the fuck are you?"

He turned back.

"You can find me in an underground area via a hidden zone by the Absinthe tent near Caeser's."

"Shit," I said, shocked that he could hear me. "Are you actually able to hear me? Because, if so, let me just say that you are one sick mother—"

"And, no," he interrupted, "I'm not actually speaking to you live, if you're thinking that. I just assumed you would ask the question of my location." He smiled. "In fact," he added while looking back at the tables that contained my four brothers, "this was recorded before I sent them out to the desert to confront you."

My brothers were beginning to move.

Gabe turned back to the mirror.

"Since you're watching this message," he pointed out, "it's obvious you have succeeded. I will miss your brothers, but they never would have been able to fill your shoes anyway." He then gave me a small salute and added, "See you soon, son."

CHAPTER 37

I climbed back out of the pit and rushed over to Portman. He was just sitting there sobbing. I'd never expected to see him like that. It was disturbing because he was usually so tough and strong.

"You okay?" I asked, kneeling down and checking his eyes. They were no longer dull. "Your eyes are clear."

"Where is he?" Portman whispered, looking terrified.

I assumed he meant Kevin.

"He's dead," I replied.

Portman let out a huge sigh and put his face in his hands. He was trying to hold back his tears, but the man was obviously broken. That was one more nail in the coffin of becoming too powerful. Someone like Kevin...or *me*...could really fuck up a person's life.

"The things that guy was going to do to my Claire," he said, referring to his wife. "I can't stop picturing them. It's horrible."

"They're not real, Portman," I assured him. "He used

magic on you to make you believe everything you're imagining, but none of it's true." I then pulled him to his feet and dragged him over to the pit. "He's dead. He can't do anything to Claire. I promise."

"But I can still see it. All of it."

So it *was* that fucking compelling magic again.

Kevin had to have used it on Portman to get him to come back down here. My brother must have also compelled my friend to believe some pretty horrific things about what would happen to Claire if he hadn't cooperated. Actually, knowing what little I did about Kevin, he was probably planning to do those things one way or the other. He just wanted Portman to suffer before killing him.

"I can't let her get hurt, Dex," Portman said desperately. "She's my lady, man."

That dug at me.

"Listen to me," I said, putting a serious amount of magic into my voice. "Kevin did *not* hurt Claire, and it is *impossible* for him to hurt her at all now." His breathing was ragged as his eyes opened wide. I felt my face glowing from the power. "*You* stopped Kevin from his attempts." It was a lie, yes, but I was getting good at those lately, and I wanted Portman to feel empowered, so fuck it. He needed to be able to battle against any residual magic that Kevin may have left behind. "*You* destroyed him, Portman. He has absolutely *no* power over you. When you think of him, his words, his images, or anything else related to him, you will feel strong, knowing that *you* crushed his sorry ass."

By the time I was finished, Portman looked like a man who had found a modicum of strength again.

He wiped the tears from his eyes and took a deep breath. He glanced around the area again in bewilderment.

"What happened?"

I pointed into the pit.

"You killed Kevin," I stated firmly.

"I did?"

"Yes."

"Oh." He looked to be wrestling with his mind again. "I don't remember—"

"He was about to get me," I explained, "and you pushed him into the pit." I then slapped him on his shoulder. "You *crushed* him, Portman. I owe you one."

"Yeah?" he asked, furrowing his brow deeply. Finally, he looked up. "I guess I did crush him, huh?"

"You sure did," I replied, lacing my voice with just a tiny bit of magic. "Again, I owe you one."

"No, no," he deflected my praise. "You'd have done the same for me."

"True," I agreed.

Portman pointed at the bodies in the area.

"I'll, uh…get my crew down here to clean all this up."

"Good idea."

We then set about picking up the various pieces of equipment we'd brought out, throwing them all into the duffel bags. The bags of lime weren't necessary at this point. Portman's crew would make sure there weren't any traces of my brothers splattered about.

After about fifteen minutes, we were back in the Jeep and getting ready to cruise.

"We're going to the precinct, right?" he asked, still looking somewhat unsure. "I think that's what you said."

"You are," I answered him, remembering where Gabe told me he was located. "I need you to drop me off at the Absinthe tent first, though."

"By Caesar's?"

"Unless you know of another Absinthe tent, yep."

He gave me a look that told me he was slowly getting back to being his usual self. It'd take a while, but I was confident he'd return in full force before too long.

"You know," The Admiral piped up, *"you could probably help the guy get his sex life back on track, if you did that magic thing on him and Claire."*

"What do you mean?" I said, holding back from just telling him to shut up.

"Compel them to get things going again," he said, and I swear I felt him shrug. *"They're married, so it's not like you're doing anything wrong...unless they totally hate each other or something."*

That was true.

"Based on how that dude was sobbing over the fact that his wife might be hurt," The Admiral added, *"I'm pretty sure he still loves her."*

"Wow," I replied, nearly beside myself with awe. "I had no idea you were such a romantic."

"Shut up."

I cracked a smile at that.

"Portman," I said as we headed through the dirt, back toward the main road, "were you serious about the fact that you no longer have relations with Claire?"

He gave me a sidelong glance.

"That's a weird question, Dex," he said. "I know we just went through a bonding moment and all, but that doesn't make me suddenly interested in having a pajama party, eating ice cream, talking about our girlfriends, and then watching *The Notebook* until we cry ourselves to sleep."

It was my turn to grimace at him.

"Dude, I'm trying to help you out here," I stated. "You've been married a long time, and I *know* for a fact that you love Claire." I looked back out at the upcoming road. "Unless that love died for you guys or something."

"It didn't die," he shot back. "We *do* love each other. We just stopped being intimate, is all. Things change as you age, Dex. When you're with the same person for a long time…things change." His voice sounded tired. "You'll see."

"Did you *want* them to change?" I challenged him.

He opened his mouth and then shut it again. It was clear to me that he was unhappy about the situation, but sometimes it was difficult to break down walls that had taken years to build.

Finally, he shook his head to indicate that he hadn't wanted things to change.

"Did Claire?"

"No," he stated almost immediately. "We just…" He trailed off.

"Got complacent," I finished for him. "It happens, man."

"Yeah."

This conversation was obviously making him uncomfortable, but I kind of felt like cupid at the moment. I had the unique ability right now to help him fix this issue with Claire. Based on what he was saying, they both *wanted* to be intimate again, but neither of them would make the first move.

"Why don't you call her and tell her that you love her, Portman?" I asked, putting the tiniest touch of magic in my voice. "I'm sure she'd appreciate hearing that."

"Yeah?"

"I know I would," I stated.

His face contorted. "You'd appreciate me calling to tell you that I love you?"

I rolled my eyes at him.

"Just call her!"

He sniffed and grinned for a moment. Then, after a sigh and a shrug, he pressed a button on the Jeep's console and said, "Call Claire."

The speakers played the sound of a ringing phone. It rang three times before she answered.

"Hey, baby," Claire said. *"I was just thinking of you."*

"Was out in the desert with Dex. Had to deal with some bad guys."

"Is everything okay?" she asked, sounding worried. *"You're not hurt, are you?"*

Okay, so that solidified it. They *were* still deeply in love with each other. And while it may not be my job to get them to reconnect, I was damn well going to do it anyway. If I could use this compelling magic for bad, I could certainly also use it for good.

"I'm fine, sweetheart," he answered her. "I just wanted to let you know I'd be home a little later than usual, and... that I love you."

"I love you, too."

"Okay," The Admiral chimed in, *"this is getting way too mushy for me. Do your thing already, will ya?"*

I smiled and then said, "Hi, Claire, it's Ian Dex here."

"Oh hi, Ian. I hope you're not getting my teddy bear into any mischief?"

"I'm going to puke," said The Admiral, *"and not in a good way."*

Ew.

"He's fine," I answered and then layered on the magic again. "I want both of you to listen to me very carefully. Whatever it was that stopped you from being intimate with each other, I want you to forget about. If you still truly love each other, and you truly want to be romantic with each other again, then you will both resume showing that love. Now is your chance to rekindle the fire you once had, but only if you *truly* want to. Do you both understand me?"

They did.

I dropped the magic.

"It was nice talking to you, Claire," I said after the spell settled. "I'll have Portman home to you soon."

"The sooner the better," she whispered in a seductive voice that even a succubus would appreciate. *"The sooner the better."*

Portman adjusted in his seat.

So did I.

CHAPTER 38

After Portman dropped me off at the tent, he headed back to the station. At least, that's what I assumed he did. I hadn't put any magic in my request, though, so he might have run home for a quickie with Claire.

Either way was fine with me.

My goal was to finish this job on my own anyway. Besides, it wasn't like my crew couldn't track me if they wanted to. My connector showed my location no matter where I was, assuming I was topside and there wasn't interference.

"*Lydia,*" I called back as I reached out with my magic, looking for the hidden zone Gabe had mentioned, "*has the crew come back yet?*"

"*No, darlin',*" she replied.

They must have been having a wonderful time with the valkyries. That was good. I'd rather that than them facing their demise against the likes of Gabe and his goons.

"*Good,*" I said. "*I mean...I'm sure they'll be back soon.*"

"*Is everything all right, puddin'?*"

"*It's peachy, babe,*" I replied, having sensed the hidden zone. "*Just found out where those wizards are holed up. Going in to have a quick chat with them now.*"

"*Won't that be dangerous?*"

"*Nah. I'm sure it was all just a simple misunderstanding.*"

"*Oh, okay.*"

"*I should be back in an hour or two,*" I added, knowing I was pushing the truth envelope a bit. "*Then I'll meet with the Directors just like I promised you I would.*"

"*Be careful, please,*" she said, sounding concerned.

"*Always am, baby.*"

CHAPTER 39

After a quick scan of the area, I stepped into the hidden zone and saw an access panel on the ground. There was a post with a console next to it, standing about waist high.

I walked over and looked at it but refrained from touching it because there were two small runes on either side.

They were protected.

Calling on what I'd learned from Warren, I concentrated on seeing through the wrapping until I spotted that one was meant for notification and the other was a shocker. These were the most common runes around access points, so I should have known that, but I wanted to make sure.

Since they were protected, I couldn't just undraw them like I'd done that night at Tommy Rocker's. I'd have to pick the lock on them first. The struggle with that was that I had no stick with me.

"I can do it, man," announced The Admiral. *"I know I can!"*

I sighed.

"And how weird is that going to look?" I countered. *"While we both know that I'll be using you to crack this lock, the rest of the world will just see me standing by a post as I swing my dick around."*

"You're in a hidden zone, dude," he pointed out.

"Oh, yeah," I said.

Then, against my better judgment, I unzipped my PPD suit and took The Admiral out.

"Ahhh," he said. *"Nice night!"*

"Shut up."

I pointed him at the first rune and started working through the sequence. A moment later, the runes disappeared and the console went full green.

"Did I do that?" asked The Admiral.

"I doubt it," I responded.

"Please put away your penis, son," a familiar voice said through the speaker on the console. *"Honestly, I expected you to have better manners than that."*

The trapdoor clicked, made a depressurization sound, and then opened.

I backed away, zipping up my pants, after tucking The Admiral safely back inside.

I took one last look around the area, sighed, and then began climbing down the steep stairs hidden there.

CHAPTER 40

̶≥

The entire area opened up when I reached the bottom of the stairs, and it all looked quite familiar.

This was the place that I had seen in a few of the *Flashes* episodes I'd experienced over the months. It was clearly different than the one I'd had with Shitfaced Fred. That one had happened in the old war.

I stood straight up at the memory.

Did that mean that the soldier who had shot Fred's master was Gabe? And what did Gabe have to do with *Shitfaced Fred* anyway?

Something told me I'd be finding out those answers, and more, soon, but not until I reached the final leg of this journey that Gabe had set out before me. I couldn't help but wonder how long all of this had been going on.

There was a door to my left and one to the right. I'd already been through the one on my left multiple times during those *Flashes* events, so I decided to see what was behind the other one.

It was locked.

I waited for it to open.

It didn't.

I knocked.

There was no answer.

Okay, so Gabe wanted me to crack the code? I wasn't exactly good at that sort of thing, so fortunately I had Turbo's skeleton key.

I rubbed my fingers together as I held my nose and the tiny key appeared from my skin. At least *some* things went smoothly in this world. The key appeared far too tiny to be of any use, but as soon as it was within the distance of the keypad, a light pulsed and I heard tumblers fall into place. I guess that saying "It's not the size, but how you use it" fit well for Turbo's key.

The handle never turned, but the door clicked open.

I walked inside and found an enormous room that seemed empty. It had a ceiling that stood some thirty feet high, which was pretty incredible considering I hadn't walked down *that* many steps. The walls were barren and the place was dimly lit.

"Well done," said the familiar voice of Gabe, who began rising out of the floor near the middle of the large space.

He clapped his hands twice and the lights came on in full. I squinted at that. With all of this advanced magic and technology, Gabe relied on *The Clapper* to manage the lights?

"I suppose I should have known it was you all along," I

said, feeling like those meetings I'd had with the man at the Three Angry Wives Pub were a major clue. "Why else would you have helped me?"

"There could have been any number of reasons," he replied.

I honestly wanted to just launch a magical barrage at him, blowing his stupid ass to bits, but I needed answers first. If I killed him now, I'd never know the truth. Part of me kind of preferred that, if I was being honest, but having spent the entirety of my life lost and not knowing who I truly was gave me pause.

"I'm sure you have many questions," he said somewhat smugly, "so feel free to ask away."

"Did you create all the ubers I faced?" I asked with some hesitation.

There were probably better questions to ask at that point, but those ubers had caused a lot of damage and had cost many lives. Knowing the truth behind their existence would help me better paint a picture of my 'father.'

Yes, I was keeping with the hand-quotes around him for now.

Gabe crossed his hands behind his back.

"Some were created, yes," he answered. "Others were merely enhanced, having lived full lives already but seeking more power all the same."

"Did you send them to attack me?"

"Yes."

That's where my brain cramped. Why the hell would he give me hints and abilities to defeat the very damn things he sent to destroy me?

"Why?"

"Because you needed to be brought out of your shell," he answered. "It had to be done over time or you wouldn't have been able to handle it. Plus, you would have been discovered much too young, and that would not have done at all." He let that sink in for a moment before adding, "Each ubernatural you defeated served to unlock pieces of your genetic code. That allowed me to gradually further your power."

"But the vampire, he—"

"Belonged to me, yes," Gabe answered. "Do you remember the blue liquid you saw me inject into your brothers during your last *Flashes* event?"

I nodded dumbly.

"That was only one tenth of the venom I put into you via Sylvester. What you have flowing through your veins is far stronger than your brothers could have ever handled."

"But why?" I asked again, trying desperately to understand all of this. "I don't get it."

"Honestly, son," he said after glancing at his watch, "the entirety of this story will take me too long to explain. Call on *Flashes* again and everything will be revealed within seconds." He gave me an encouraging nod. "Don't worry, I'll wait."

With a strong sense of trepidation, I closed my eyes.

Flashes.

CHAPTER 41

I didn't recognize the faces I was seeing because they were going through that same mist crap that happened when I was sitting in the room with the Directors. Glimpses came through, but they disappeared just as fast, leaving nothing but a hazed memory that faded like a dream.

But the voices...

I recognized those voices.

Some of them, anyway.

"And you're certain this will work?" asked O.

"It will take time and research," Gabe replied, "but I'm confident, yes. There have already been numerous tests done to show that our level of genetic engineering is beyond anything ever previously imagined."

Gabe was seated in much the same way I was during my meetings with the Directors, but this felt more like a congressional hearing. There were many bodies around the table in front of him, and they were all intently listening and asking questions.

"How have you managed testing?" asked someone whose voice I didn't know. "Did you do it on supers, normals, or animals?"

"All three," Gabe replied. "In every case, the tests have shown remarkable results."

A slew of other questions followed, but I was fast-forwarded through most of them.

"The question on the minds of the Paranormal Police Department," Silver chimed in as the speed of the replay returned to normal, "is whether or not we'll be able to *safely* utilize these enhanced officers to police our streets." He paused. "Will we?"

"In time," Gabe replied with a nod. "I firmly believe this is doable. I also believe this is the *only* way we'll be able to stop the spread of supernatural villainy."

Unless Gabe was showing me the script he wanted me to see, doctored to make him look good, it seemed he was genuinely interested in keeping the public safe. But if that was the case, why would he have created someone like Kevin? And why would there be all these ubers, that *he* created, attacking the world like this?

"If we approve utilizing these test subjects of yours in the field," asked Zack, "how can we be assured of a failsafe in the event that they malfunction?"

"Each of them has only a single genetic enhancement," Gabe answered. "Therefore, they can be taken down by those who are not part of their kind."

This sounded like he was just talking about the

standard upgrades that the PPD cops got now. If it wasn't, the Directors would have had more concerns…right?

∽

Everything went dark and then slowly faded back into view. Years had apparently passed as the decor and technology looked quite a bit different than the last time. Plus, the panel was smaller than before.

"…Yes," the voice of O was saying, "we agree that the individual enhancements have been quite successful, but you are now talking about turning already powerful supernaturals into something far beyond that."

"It's no different, sir," stated Gabe. "It's merely the necessary evolution of the technology. The officers program that we implemented ten years ago has cut supernatural crime by nearly seventy percent across the board." He put up his hands. "What I'm promising now is a one-hundred-percent drop in crime."

"Yes," agreed Zack, "but at what cost?"

"Agreed, Zack," stated Silver.

"Now, wait a second," EQK said in his snippy voice. "If this butt fucker can guarantee wiping out crime completely, why do you two jizz slurpers want to stop him?"

"Please refrain from calling members of the panel names, EQK," O said in a tired voice. "Oh, and our esteemed Mr. Dexington as well."

Dexington?

My name was really Ian Dexington?

That was just awful.

"Fuck you, O," EQK responded without malice. "We've got this dick brain over here giving us a way to wipe out crime, and there's a bunch of hippies on the panel crying about it. Maybe you've all come down with a ripping case of vaginitis?"

The event fast-forwarded again.

"We approve the use of genetic enhancements to bring *one* individual to the state of what we will call 'ubernatural,' Mr. Dexington," O said, acting as the voice for the rest of the committee. "We expect to be kept completely up-to-date on each step of the process."

∽

"...But I just need a little more time," Gabe pleaded. "This is a new science. It takes trials to be sure that it works properly."

"You blew up half of Manhattan, you clit smacker," EQK roared, "and you used a fucking pixie to do it!"

I had to wonder if the pixie that EQK was referring to was none other than Rot, the guy I had battled in a *Joke-off* a couple of months back.

"I admit that's true, Director EQK," Gabe replied coolly, "but we were able to subdue him rather quickly, and we are making strides to correct the issue that caused him to become unsettled."

"Unfortunately, Mr. Dexington," Silver argued, "this is the fifth time in as many months that we've heard this exact testimony from you."

"But, you must see—"

"See what?" Zack interrupted. "The only thing I see is that thousands of lives have been lost. Your Frankenstein monsters are not working, Mr. Dexington."

"I would have to agree," O noted.

It fast-forwarded again.

"All in favor of shutting down this program, please vote 'aye,'" called O.

Everyone voted in the affirmative.

"You have thirty days to shut down the program, Mr. Dexington," commanded O. Then he softened a bit. "We all know that you have done your best here, Gabe. Your heart was in the right place the entire time, but we just can't risk any more lives being lost."

∼

We were back in the lab now. There were tunnels being carved out, mostly through the use of magic by people I'd seen before.

There was Reese the mage, Shitfaced Fred the necromancer, Charlotte the dragon, Rex the werewolf, Rot the pixie, and Sylvester the vampire. There were many others, too, but I didn't recognize most of them.

The magic-users were carving out tunnels faster than anything I'd ever seen before. The others were carrying gear down and placing it in a large room. As Gabe scanned the area, I noted that it was the same place Gabe and I were standing in *outside* of *Flashes* right now. The difference was that this room wasn't currently empty.

"Keep digging here," Gabe commanded. "We're going to head back for another round of equipment. We'll return soon."

Everything sped forward, showing a quick trip as a convoy of vans and trucks cruised out to the middle of the desert. Just as they were about to turn off the main road, a building in the distance exploded.

"Bastards," Gabe hissed after a moment. "They were going to kill me and all of my creations."

I had the distinct impression that the 'they' in that statement referred to the Directors.

"They'll pay for that."

~

Two children were in incubators. One male and one female. They were both sleeping as IVs dripped bluish liquid into their veins.

On the front of one was the name 'Ian,' the other said, 'Wynn.'

'Wynn Dexington' wasn't as fucked up as Wynn Dex, but it was still pretty fucked up.

"Okay, my little amalgamites," Gabe said as he tapped the table that housed both my sister and me, "you are the future of the world." He glanced over at four young boys who were lying on a nearby table. "Your brothers will one day help in your growth, but they just aren't quite up to spec for what I need. Once you have reached your full potential, the world will finally be a safe place." He sighed heavily. "However, I will have to choose one of you to stay while the other goes out and grows up as an innocent."

He pulled out a coin.

"Heads, and Wynn goes; tails, and it will be Ian."

We all know how that turned out.

~

Over the next few minutes, I saw wisps of my life as Gabe paid various families money to raise me, each unlocking a part of my potential before moving me on to the next set of foster parents.

That meant that *none* of them had ever truly cared about me.

They were simply hired guns.

Watching this was certainly *not* making me feel very warm and fuzzy toward Gabe. In fact, I was of the mind to kick his ass all over the place at the moment. Unfortunately, I had no control over his body, or I'd have had him punch himself right in the nuts.

The scenes continued, one after the other, until I finally landed as the chief of the PPD in Vegas.

~

"And now you will all be sent out to do what you were intended to do," Gabe was saying to all of the ubers in the room. "You will each prepare and be ready the moment I call you."

One hand went up.

"Yes, Reese?"

"What is our ultimate goal, sir?"

"You will destroy the evil one known as Ian Dex."

Everything began to fade as three powerful words began to form inside my mind.

What.

The.

Fuck?

CHAPTER 42

I snapped out of *Flashes* and just stared at Gabe for a few seconds. I had no words. He *wanted* them to kill his own son? For some reason, this just didn't sit well with me, especially since I'd been dumped into the system for my entire life as part of some grand training program.

What kind of parent does that?

"I know what you're thinking," Gabe said. "How could I have possibly let the Directors strong-arm me the way they did, right?"

"That's not even close to what I was thinking," I answered.

"Oh?"

"I was thinking something more along the lines of how you could be such a fucking asshole?" I spat. "And then I started thinking about the best way to kill you for being such a fucking asshole."

He bridled at my response.

Good.

"You will show me respect, Ian," he hissed.

"Why would I do that?" I asked with a laugh. "Because you're my 'father'?" Yes, I *did* use air quotes that time. "I'm nothing but a goddamn experiment to you, Gabe...or did you want me to call you Dad, or maybe Daddy?" I then grimaced. "Okay, I'm *not* calling you Daddy. That's just weird."

"*Agreed,*" noted The Admiral.

Gabe took a few deep breaths, visibly trying to calm himself. I guess he wasn't used to having kids who talked back to him. What was he going to do, though, give me a timeout?

"You *saw* what happened, Ian," he said, keeping his voice steady. "The Directors cut my ability to continue the single most important scientific breakthrough in the history of our world." His fists were squeezing rhythmically. "Then they tried to kill me and my creations out of fear that I would pursue my chosen path without regard to their damnable rules and ethics."

"Which you absolutely did," I pointed out while giving him a they-were-right-to-do-so look.

"But they couldn't have known I was planning to do that," he countered, "which meant that they had decided to kill me before I'd even had the chance to shut things down."

That was a stretch.

The Directors weren't exactly on my Christmas-card list at the moment, but I doubted they'd just blow up a building they knew was full of people just because they wanted to silence them.

Then again, maybe they would.

All right, so the jury was out on that, but it didn't fix the bit about my 'father' being a bloody psychotic.

"Fuck them," I said, referring to the Directors. "What I want to know is why *you* told the ubers to kill me?"

"Ah, yes, that," he said, nodding. "I can understand that you may have found that part somewhat upsetting."

"A little bit, yep."

"I knew they didn't have a chance against you," he explained. "Well, assuming you rose to the challenge and became what I knew you could be, anyway."

"Meaning you *didn't* know if they had a chance against me or not," I corrected him. "Basic logic, Gabe."

He bowed slightly. "Let's just say we are living in the land of odds, and I was confident with my bet."

I rolled my eyes at him.

"As I explained before, each uber I sent your way unlocked more and more of you," he continued, "but I wasn't pleased with the speed at which you were growing." He began to pace back and forth. "Fortunately, Officer Cress decided to leave the precinct. That was perfect because it put you in an emotional state. All I had to do was work to bring you out of your shell even further."

"So, wait, *you* had Rex kidnap Rachel?"

"Correct," he replied as if it were nothing. "That started you down a path of both anger and vulnerability. From there, I just needed to push a few more buttons before having you injected with venom."

Well, that about settled the debate over Gabe being a raving lunatic or not.

Then again, maybe all parents did shit like this to their kids? I didn't really have much of a reference point aside from shows like *The Brady Bunch*, and I had a difficult time believing that was even remotely realistic.

As an aside, am I the only one who preferred Jan over Marsha?

"*Loved those braces,*" The Admiral sighed wistfully.

"Anyway," I said, shaking myself back to the moment, "you essentially fucked with me my entire life, and now you want me to embrace you with open arms? Uh, no." I then leaned in a bit and added, "That's the summary from my side, if you give a shit."

He blinked stoically. "Sometimes we must make sacrifices for the greater good, son."

"Quit it with the 'son' stuff, will you?" I rasped. "And sacrifices are fine *if* you know you're making them *and* if you agree with the cause in the first place."

His expression changed to one of concern.

"I'm assuming you *do* agree with how well you turned out?" he asked. "Can crime continue in Las Vegas now that you have the powers I've given you?"

Technically, crime could continue just fine, but he had a point. It'd only be a matter of time before word got out that I was now a major badass. Once that happened, only supers who had a death wish would fuck with my town.

"Okay, I'll give you that one, but I have a feeling you're not planning to stop there."

"Of course not," he replied, rubbing his hands together like a maniacal evil genius. Technically, I guess that's precisely what he was. "Between me, you, and Wynn, we will grow an entirely new batch of amalgamites. Then we'll distribute them throughout the world and everyone will follow *my* rule of law without question."

That caused an eyebrow to raise.

"*Your* rule of law?"

His face twitched slightly.

"You know what I mean."

"Yeah," I agreed with a heavy dose of sarcasm, "I really do."

"Good." His smile was wide and proud. "Soon, the world will bow to the Dexingtons."

I grunted and then cracked my neck from side to side. Things were about to go south for old Gabe. I still couldn't believe this guy was my dear old dad.

"How come my brothers thought their last name was Dex?" I asked. "I mean, I get why you did that with me, but why them?"

"In case they were captured, of course."

"Ah, right." That's when a thought struck me. "What about…Mom?"

"Mom?"

"Yeah, what happened to her? Is she still around?"

"You didn't technically have a mother," he answered, looking a bit uncomfortable. "There was an egg, certainly, but it was chosen at random. I fertilized the egg using genetically altered sperm that contained DNA adjustments and additions from various supernatural donors. The only one you didn't get was dragon. It was just too complicated and risky."

"So you made me out of jizz soup?"

He frowned. "That is a juvenile way to put it, but essentially yes."

"Which means that *you* aren't technically my father."

"My sperm was part of the concoction, and I *did* raise you."

"No, you didn't," I shot back. "You paid others to raise me."

"Technicalities," he said, waving a dismissive hand at me. "You *are* my son and together we *will* rule the world."

There he went again with the megalomaniac talk.

I was sure that his heart had been in the right place all those years ago when this all started, but it was clear that Gabe's power exploded his ego somewhere along the way. Regardless, it was clear that he had no doubt that running the world under *his* 'law' was for the best. Dictators tended to get pretty fucked in the head over time.

> *Great men are almost always bad men, even when they exercise influence and not authority, still more when you superadd the tendency or the certainty of corruption by authority.*
>
> *- Lord Acton*

Again, I watched a lot of documentaries.

"Here's the thing, Pop," I said, realizing the shit was about to hit the fan, "I think you've lost touch with reality a bit, and I'm not about to back the next Hitler or Stalin."

He went to open his mouth and then grimaced.

"Don't you think you're being somewhat dramatic, son?"

"Says the guy who just announced that he wanted to rule the world?" I scoffed. "You've lost your marbles, old man. Worse, I was damn close to implicitly trusting you, but…"

I just shook my head.

He closed his eyes and took in a long, slow breath.

"I understand that you may be somewhat upset," he said in a diplomatic tone of voice, "but that will soon pass."

"Even if it did, I'm not going to be a part of your draconian plans."

His eyes creased and his skin flushed. Obviously, Gabe was not a fan of the way I viewed his chosen path.

"You *will* be a part of my plans, Ian Rupert Dexington, or you *will* be killed."

My jaw hung open.

"My middle name is fucking 'Rupert'?"

I then jolted again at the breadth of what he'd just said to me.

"And, secondly," I added, "did you seriously just do the parent thing where you called me by my full name?"

His face was so tight it looked to have been chiseled from granite.

"I have no more time for games," he announced. "I have invested heavily into you over the years, both financially and emotionally. But you are a grown man now. You may choose to do as you please." He stared at me. "What will it be, son? Do you plan to cast aside your pointless emotions and follow me now, or will you choose to die?"

"Well, when you put it like that," I said, shaking my head sadly, "I guess I'll have to die, then."

"Excellent," he said. "Finally, some sense..." He then glanced up at me, looking baffled. "What?"

"I'm not going to help you, Gabe," I stated firmly. "In fact, I'm going to do everything within my power to stop you."

The look on his face was a mixture of sadness and irritation.

"Pity."

CHAPTER 43

*T*he one thing I wasn't sure of was how my sister fit in to all of this. If it was just me against Gabe, I was cool with that, but Wynn was probably a lot like me, meaning she'd be tough to beat.

On top of that, I had no idea what other tricks Gabe had up his sleeve. I doubted he was unprepared, though. He just wasn't the type.

Still, I *was* taken by surprise when he sprouted fangs and long, sharp fingernails.

Even more surprising was that my fangs and nails popped out a moment later. It was as if he could control what my body was doing, too. That was my guess anyway, seeing that *I* sure as hell didn't purposefully dive into vampire mode.

"I will battle you with each fathet of our genetic makeup," he declared, demonstrating that he, too, had yet to master the vampire lisp. "Thith will demonthtrate to you firththand that you cannot win againtht me."

"Wait," I said, "are you thaying that you're an amalgamite altho?"

"Yeth," he replied. "My path wath not as eathy ath yourth, though. I had to thuffer through the entire protheth ath an adult. It wath…difficult."

He lunged at me, raking his claws at my head in a burst of speed that caught me off guard. One of his nails connected, slicing its way across my temple, causing blood to pour into my left eye.

I swung back, but he jumped away before I could connect. If he continued moving at this speed, I'd be dead in no time.

Then, he leaped backward and turned into a werewolf. It happened all in one motion. Smooth. I'd dare say, he'd practiced. Then again, if that were the case, why wouldn't he have practiced speaking without a lisp when in fanged mode?

The other thing I noticed was that he didn't howl.

There was no time to think about that right now, because my body twisted, sending shocks of pain radiating through every fiber of my being.

My howl was intense.

Too bad it was silenced by the crushing blow of Gabe plowing into me, knocking me flat on my ass. Then, my belly exposed, he went to wrap his massive jaws around my throat.

Uh…no.

I kicked up, sending him flying overhead as I struggled to get back to my feet.

We both spun to face each other at the same time,

growling and showing our teeth like a couple of Rottweilers who were fighting over the same treat.

His eyes flashed.

He was going werebear, and that meant I was too.

As if the pain of turning into full wolf wasn't bad enough, going full werebear was fucking ridiculous. I finally understood why Portman was gruff and often grumpy.

That shit was unbearably painful.

Gabe and I collided, tearing at each other with massive paws and teeth. Our roars were so loud that I wouldn't have been surprised to learn the people in the Absinthe tent above us heard us.

We wrestled for a solid minute, neither of us getting ahead of the other. Sure, there were bites, and slashes, and plenty of blood, but nothing that either of us couldn't withstand.

Gabe pushed away and changed again.

This time, into a pixie.

CHAPTER 44

I'd never seen the world from such a vantage point. Everything was gigantic. The already large room appeared multiple times larger than before.

"What the fuck?" I said, looking at my hands.

"Quiet, you penis-hole taster!" Gabe demanded.

It was really strange hearing him talk that way, but I did take some solace in that he didn't seem to be very good at it.

"What's your plan now, cum donut?" I asked. "Are we going to race around the room or something?"

"No, you gargantuan taint stain," he replied, crossing his little arms. "We're going to have a *Joke-off!*"

Oh, goodie.

I'd wiped up an *actual* pixie at this not long ago. Somehow I thought Gabe wasn't going to have a chance. He was too proper. Of course, that could also prove to be a problem for me since *Joke-offs* required the other side to laugh in order for the current joke-teller to get a point.

Gabe was not one who seemed prone to jocularity.

"Fine," I said, feeling weird at hearing my voice sounding so small and tinny. "What kind of jokes are we going to do?"

"Free-for-all," Gabe replied.

"I didn't know that was an option."

"It's my game, pube-comber," he sneered. "That means we play by my rules."

Gabe clearly had a thing about people playing by *his* rules.

"Okay," I started. "A guy is at the shrink's office in the middle of a session. The shrink pulls out a bunch of cards that have inkblots all over them."

"A Rorschach test," affirmed Gabe. "Go on."

"Right, well, the doctor tells the patient to say the first thing that comes to mind upon seeing each picture." I cleared my throat. "He shows the first one and the patient says, 'That's a guy and a girl doing it on the bed.' The doctor shows the second one and the guy remarks, 'That's a guy and a girl doing it on the kitchen table.' The doctor says, 'Hmmm,' and shows another image. This time the patient says, 'That's a guy and a girl doing it on a park bench.' The doctor finally sets the cards down and remarks, 'I think I know what your problem is. All you think about is sex.' The patient looks affronted at this diagnosis and shoots back, 'Hey, Doc, they're *your* pictures!'"

Gabe didn't even crack a smile.

"Tough crowd," I mumbled. "Right, well, your turn."

"A three-legged dog walked into a pub in the Old

West," Gabe began. "He scanned the room with menace and said, 'I'm looking for the man who shot my paw.'"

I didn't laugh.

I *did* do a facepalm, but that didn't count as points against.

"What did Cinderella do when she got to the ball?" I asked.

Gabe tapped his chin for a moment. "What?"

"Gagged."

Again, nothing.

In fact, he didn't even wait a beat before starting in on his next joke.

"How do snails fight?" he asked me.

I shrugged in response.

"They slug it out."

Okay, so he was going for the *really* corny jokes. That made me think that those were the kind that made him laugh. So…

"What do you call a guy with a rubber toe?"

"Hmmm," he mused. "I don't know."

"Roberto."

It started as a twinkle in his eye, then turned to a grin, jumping next into a full-blown smile, and finally laughter ensued.

Right, so corny jokes were where it was at with him.

Unfortunately, he caught on quickly that I'd just bested him. His laughter stopped abruptly and he snapped his fingers, bringing himself back to his normal look and size.

I returned moments later, happy to find that my PPD

suit was still in almost perfect shape. Obviously these things were magically imbued.

"I'll give it to you that you *were* the better pixie," he admitted. "I have never been one who excelled in humor."

"Nooo," I said, layering on so much sarcasm that it even made *me* feel I was being a bit douchey. "But you're sooo good at it."

"I sense your sarcasm," he said, his voice just above a simmer. "No matter. We'll now joust in something I *know* I'll beat you at."

"Being a dick?"

"Exact— What?"

"Nothing," I replied. "You were saying?"

His hands began to glow.

CHAPTER 45

Fire struck against my shield with such power that I thought certain I was going to be fried to a crisp, but it held.

There may have been a fair bit of yelling coming from my side, though. It wasn't the kind of yelling that you'd hear someone belt out due to fear, it was the kind that said, "Youuuu shallll notttt passss!"

After what felt like an eternity, Gabe stopped his flow of magic. That gave me time to drop my shield and let my energy fly.

There was no more holding back, either.

"You wanted to unleash the Kracken, Pop?" I barked at him. "Well, here it comes, motherfucker!"

I gave it everything I had, and then some.

I'd never felt power like this. And with each casting, it seemed to grow stronger and stronger.

My mages all got more and more tired as they fired off spells.

I didn't.

My rage spilled forth like lava.

There was no pain.

Just pure, white-hot menace, and it felt terrifyingly wonderful.

I cackled like a madman as I walked around Gabe, throwing spell after spell at him, doing everything I could to destroy that son of a bitch.

"Yes," he yelled over the noise, his shield somehow managing to contain my best. "You are growing, my son!"

That statement kicked the wind right out of my sails.

I stopped.

"What?"

"The more you use your power," he said, his crazy-eyed face full of the same hate I was also feeling, "the more intoxicating it will be."

My anger began to fade instantly as I looked around the room, down at my hands, and across at the man who was the impetus for all this insanity.

He was right.

It happened when I used compelling magic, it happened when I cast even the smallest of spells, and it was *seriously* happening when I threw massive ones like I'd just done against him.

I dropped my hands by my side.

"You're a real piece of shit, Gabe," I said, shaking my head. "You're like the Darth Vader to my Luke Skywalker."

"Huh?"

"You fucked with my life since I was born and now you're trying to completely change who I've become."

"Oh, please," Gabe said, looking up at the ceiling.

"You've had cars, clothes, a great place to live, and you've got more money than most CEOs in this country."

I hated it when people pointed that out to me. Yes, it was true, but problems were relative. I'd have despised Gabe's sorry ass even if I'd been destitute growing up.

"I'm not going to help you," I said in a cold voice. "You may do your worst to me, but I'm done here."

The look on his face was priceless. Years of research, waiting, pushing buttons, and releasing ubers on me had clearly failed.

He had failed.

I crossed my arms. "The one thing you didn't plan for, Pop, was how so many decent people over the years would influence my personality."

His eyes were burning, but they eventually cooled.

"Then there is nothing more I can do for you," he whispered sadly. "After I kill you, your sister and I will rule the world. It's a shame, boy, but I have no stomach for weak-minded fools."

"Before you go and put me out of my misery, Pop," I said, holding up a finger, "I just wanted you to know that I'll be forever grateful for one thing that you *did* give me throughout all of this."

He tilted his head as his hands dripped flames.

"And what is that?" he asked in condescending fashion.

"*Time.*"

His eyes shot open an instant before his world slowed. There was nothing he could do now, though, because I had the element of speed on my side.

Gabe was the one who had warned me not to use the *Time* power word unless it was absolutely necessary.

There were only three uses available of it, after all.

I'd called on the first one during Dr. Vernon's awesome orgasm, the second one when we'd faced Charlotte in the Badlands, and now this.

It seemed fitting that Gabe was going to bite it due to this gift he'd given me—or was it a curse? I supposed it depended on one's perspective.

Right now, I'd call it a gift.

I rushed over to him as his face continued to slowly contort into something that was beyond hate.

"Sorry, Pop," I whispered, "but you're just too much of a shit to be allowed to live."

With that, I bypassed magic completely, having the sneaking suspicion that it might backfire on me. Knowing Gabe, that was a definite possibility.

Instead, I took out Boomy, stuck it under his chin, and ended his sorry ass.

But the fun didn't end there.

The moment Gabe hit the floor, a swelling of magic began building up around his body like some type of self-destruct mechanism.

Time ceased a moment later, returning the world around me to its normal speed.

I glanced back at the door, seeing how far I was from it. That explained why this room had been so goddamn big. Gabe wanted to make sure that if *he* didn't win, *I* sure as hell wouldn't either.

My legs pumped with everything I had, but there was no chance.

I couldn't escape it.

It was not the kind of explosion you'd expect from a

bomb, though. I didn't fly across the room and slam into a wall and there weren't any concussive effects. In fact, there wasn't even a sound.

The magic merely shredded the layers of venomous power I had throughout my body. I *felt* wave after wave fading away, piece by piece, until there was nothing left but who I was before the infamous Sylvester biting event.

I was drowning in anguish, like someone had given me the most tremendous high of a lifetime and then snatched it away, leaving me in a state of horrendous withdrawal.

Finally, I crashed to the ground, fading in and out of consciousness.

My groans were so weak, it was hard to tell that they even belonged to me. But seeing as though I was the only live body in this room...

Footsteps sounded.

Okay, so maybe I *wasn't* the only live body in this room.

Shit.

I fought to open my eyes, to stay conscious, but it was damn near impossible. My brain just refused to cooperate.

But then I felt a set of hands lift up my head, sending a wave of power into me, bringing my mind back online slightly.

Hers was the face of an angel.

She had black hair and hazel eyes. Her skin was olive and as smooth as silk. Unlike my brothers, though, she looked finished...like she had a soul or whatever the hell you wanted to call it.

"Wynn," I rasped as she continued her curious study of my face, "is that you?"

"Yes," she replied. "And you are Ian. I have studied you alongside Father for years."

"Yes."

"You have killed him," she said without inflection, no anger in her voice. "I was unable to do so."

I swallowed. "Got lucky, I guess."

"Yes," she agreed.

"But now that he's gone," I promised her, "we can be a family. A real family."

She smirked as a wave of evil caressed her eyes.

"I'm afraid that won't work for me," she said. "With you out of the way, I'll be free to run Father's...*my* empire without interference."

"But..." I started, but I trailed off as she dropped my head on the hard floor, bringing the haze back to full.

"Time to die, brother," she whispered in my ear.

"Back off, bitch," came a louder voice, one that I'd heard many times over the years. "Do it now or you'll be so fucking full of holes that you'll look like a goddamn springboard."

Rachel Cress had entered the room.

CHAPTER 46

Wynn stood up and looked across at my officers. I couldn't see them, but I knew they were all there.

They had to be.

Everything went dark for a moment and then came back.

I was clearly fading in and out of consciousness at this point.

"We'll meet again, brother," Wynn said, giving me a gentle kick to the stomach. "Mark my words on that."

Then she turned and walked away.

The next time my eyes opened, I saw Rachel kneeling next to me.

"Babe," she said, slapping my face lightly, "are you there? Come on! Answer me!"

"I'm here," I said through ragged breaths. "I'll be fine. I just need to rest."

"So you're okay, then?" she asked, the look of concern grave on her face. "You're going to make it?"

"Yes," I answered, already feeling the healing effects of my body underway. "I just need time."

"Good," Rachel said, drawing her fist back. "You son of a bitch."

The punch cracked me square in the jaw, turning the world black again.

CHAPTER 47

The next time I awoke, I was in the hospital. My entire team was in there with me, and they didn't look happy.

Rachel walked over to my bedside.

"Are you okay?" she asked.

I pulled my hands up to protect myself.

"Yes."

She rolled her eyes at me and grunted. Then, without much effort, she pulled my arms out of the way.

"Why did you do it?" she asked.

I knew what she was talking about, of course. Why did I leave them all behind while I went out and fought this battle alone? They knew the answer to the question already, but they clearly wanted to hear it from my lips.

"Because you'd all have been killed," I said.

"That wasn't your choice to make."

"It damn well *was* my choice to make, Rachel," I shot back in a raspy voice, pushing her away from me.

"Whether or not you all like it, *I* am the chief of the Las Vegas Paranormal Police Department. That means that *I* have to make decisions from time to time that you will not like."

I was starting to feel like one of the Directors at that point.

Maybe this was the kind of thing they dealt with at their level?

Damn it.

I had to tone it down a bit. Not only was I being a dick, but my head was threatening to explode.

"Look," I said more quietly, "you're my team. I know each of your strengths and weaknesses." I glanced over at Warren. "Most of you, anyway. The point is that you would have all been killed. I *know* this to be true," I stated emphatically. "And you three mages know it as well. You admitted that you wouldn't have a chance against me when I was in full power. What would you have done against six of me?"

"Six?" asked Griff.

"My father, sister, and four brothers," I said. "And, by now, I'm assuming you know that Gabe was my father?"

They nodded.

I looked from face to face.

"You would have all died," I reiterated. "Now, you can hate me as much as you want, but at least you're able to do that because of the decision I made."

There was nothing more to be said. They knew I hadn't made my choice lightly, and they knew they would have certainly been killed if they'd have joined me in this fight.

"You're still an asshole," Rachel grunted.

"Worse than that, babe," I replied, certain she wasn't about to be happy about my next proclamation, "I no longer have those uber powers. They got wiped out after I killed Gabe."

"None of them?" she asked, her eyes distraught. "There has to be at least *something* left."

"Actually," I said, frowning, "I don't really know."

With a grunt, I pushed and my fangs popped out.

"Aw, thit."

CHAPTER 48

The Directors were already there when I'd arrived. My body was mostly healed, but I was definitely exhausted.

Regardless, this was the moment I'd been waiting for.

"Mr. Dex," O said, breaking the ice, "we're glad to see you are doing well."

"Thank you."

"We obviously have many questions," he continued, "but we want to first give you the opportunity to tell us what you know."

I smiled and looked away for a moment. There was so much I could tell them, but they knew all of it already. Well, *most* of it anyway.

"Let's just say that I'm *fully* aware of who created me," I said. "I'm also aware of *why* he created me, what his plans were, and also his history."

There was a moment of silence.

"Kind of feels like getting caught with your hand in the

cookie jar, doesn't it?" I asked, but I got no response. "What you *don't* know is that there were quite a few more ubers created. He'd moved before you guys tried to destroy him."

"You must understand that—"

"Oh, I understand, Director Zack," I interrupted. "You were doing what you thought was right. You were trying to save countless lives from the designs of a madman."

"Yes," Zack whispered.

"And I'm sure *you* understand that Gabe was trying to accomplish the same thing." I crossed my legs, which didn't feel great since I was still admittedly very sore. "The difference between you and him is that..." I sighed. "The difference is that you were in the right."

The bottom line was that I actually felt that way. Misguided or not, the Directors had made the right choice when shutting down Gabe's work. Going in with a killing strike was probably not the best idea, but I assumed there was a reason for that as well.

At this point, I felt they at least owed me *some* honesty, though.

"Why did you blow up that building?" I asked.

"As you know, Mr. Dex," O answered, "there are some things we cannot divulge."

"Ah, bullshit," EQK stepped up to the conversation. "This prick just fucking killed Gayyyyyybe, and you're still holding on to your precious secrets?"

"EQK, now is not—"

"Kiss my tiny testicles O-gasm," EQK hissed in response. "Dex here just killed his family in order to save this town—the *world*—from being overrun. I think our sorry assess owe him a little transparency."

"I'm warning you, EQK."

"We blew up that building because we knew your foreskin of a father was a complete psycho," EQK bellowed. "We also knew that his followers were just as nuts as he was. So, we called in a strike and *kerpow*, those bitches were dead!" He then coughed. "Or so we thought."

"You are relieved of duty, EQK," O stated.

"No, wait," I called out before O could press the button. "If you kick him out, you may as well accept my resignation right now."

Again, silence.

"What are you saying, Mr. Dex?" asked Silver. "Are you giving us an ultimatum?"

"You're damn right I am," I replied, uncrossing my legs and getting to my feet. "I've spent my entire life being dicked around, gentlemen. That's going to stop. One way or the other, that's going to stop."

I looked at each of their positions, one at a time. No, I couldn't actually see them, but I wanted to make sure they could see the seriousness on my face.

"We all know EQK is a pain in the ass," I stated. "He's probably one of the biggest cock massagers I've ever met, too."

"I appreciate that," EQK said.

"But he's also stepped up to bat for me more than once," I continued. "Time for me to repay the favor."

I let that sink in for a moment.

Then, I softened a bit, but not too much.

"Guys, it comes down to this: My sister is out there,

and she's *not* a good person. Whether or not you keep me on the force, I'm going to hunt her down and I'm going to kill her."

I looked at the floor for a moment, feeling the weight of my own words.

"She's my last known living relative, but I know it has to be done."

If I was being honest right now, I'd say that I felt a lot of trepidation about what I was doing here, but I genuinely didn't feel I had much of a choice. The world had just become even more dangerous, and I was the only one who had a chance to stop the threat.

Frankly, I doubted my restricted powers would match Wynn's, but what I had was better than what anyone else had. Besides, my team of fantastic officers would stand by my side...as long as I let them.

"You need me, gentlemen," I reminded them. "Now, I'm not going to be one of those guys who manages from the bottom up just because I have leverage. You have your jobs to do and I have mine. I don't want that to change." I set my jaw. "But I will *not* play the hide-information-from-Ian game any longer. You will give me all of the information I need from this point on, without hesitation, or I will walk from this precinct."

"Fuck yeah," EQK bellowed. "Finally, Wrong Sex Dex steps up to the microphone!"

CHAPTER 49

The next night was just as beautiful as the one before. I sat out in the desert, atop a hill, staring out at the stars while thinking.

Rachel had wanted to join me for once, but I told her I needed a little time alone.

She wasn't too happy about that, but after reminding me that I had to turn in all the officer evaluations in the morning before heading off to an appointment to donate a batch of baby batter to the Netherworld weretiger restoration effort, she gave me a kiss and let me go.

Ugh.

It'd been a long year and a lot of shit had happened.

People had died, friends were hurt, relationships were strained…

But there were good things too.

Portman's marriage was back on track, for example. Plus, Rachel and I were finally in a committed relationship that looked to be running as smoothly as could be expected, especially since we were now playing with the valkyries pretty regularly.

"*Are you okay, honey?*" asked Lydia through the connector. "*I've been worried about you.*"

"*I'm fine, baby,*" I said, cracking a smile. "*Just taking a little break, is all.*"

"*Well, if you need anything, you let me know.*"

Feeling that I could *finally* say whatever I wanted around her, now that there was a newfound agreement in place with the Directors, I felt comfortable enough to open up a little more to her.

"*I'm just sitting out here looking at the stars,*" I said. "*I know things are going to get difficult soon, so I need to center myself.*"

"*I understand,*" she replied. "*Thank you for telling me that, lover.*"

"*You bet,*" I said. "*I'll talk to you later, my little digital deviant.*"

I smiled to myself, cutting off the communication as her giggle faded away.

That's when a new voice chimed in.

"*Hello, brother,*" said Wynn through my connector.

How she'd gotten through on this frequency was a mystery to me.

"*Hello, Wynn,*" I replied. "*Where are you?*"

"*To your right,*" she answered.

I looked over and saw a small light a few hills over. So she'd come out to watch the stars with me?

"*The sky is beautiful, isn't it?*" I asked.

"*Yes,*" she replied. "*I've not seen them in a long time.*"

That was sad.

Obviously, Gabe had kept her locked away from the world as he molded her into what he wanted.

Fortunately or not, Wynn and I were too far apart to do any real damage to each other, but I had the feeling that she just wanted to have a moment of family time before ending everything.

I'd be lying if I said I didn't want the same thing.

Yes, she had planned to kill me before, but that was yesterday.

She was alone now, and I was sure that fact was weighing heavily on her.

Gabe was no longer there to pull her strings and tell her what to do.

The world looked different when you were alone.

I sighed.

"It doesn't have to go this way, you know?"

"Yes, it does, brother."

I was afraid she would respond like that.

Wynn wasn't going to give up her position.

We may have been related, but we were raised in totally different ways. She would forever seek to look out for number one, just like the man who had trained her.

"That's unfortunate," I whispered. *"It's also sad that so many people are going to have to die in the process."*

"Sacrifice is necessary," she replied.

Yep, definitely her father's daughter.

"I'm going to come after you," I warned, looking back over at her. *"I have to."*

"You must follow your path, brother," she said. *"Just as I must follow mine."*

We sat in silence for the next twenty minutes, staring at the sky.

Finally, I saw movement over on her hill.

"It was nice to have this time together, brother," she said. *"I'm sorry you are unwilling to join me, but I understand your position. Please know that I will do my best to make your death as quick and painless as I can when the time comes."*

"Thanks, Wynn," I replied sadly. *"I'll do the same for you, should our roles be reversed."*

And with that, my sister disappeared into the night.

~

The End

~

Thanks for Reading

If you enjoyed this book, would you please leave a review at the site you purchased it from? It doesn't have to be a book report… just a line or two would be fantastic and it would really help us out!

John P. Logsdon
www.JohnPLogsdon.com

John was raised in the MD/VA/DC area. Growing up, John had a steady interest in writing stories, playing music, and tinkering with computers. He spent over 20 years working in the video games industry where he acted as designer and producer on many online games. He's written science fiction, fantasy, humor, and even books on game development. While he enjoys writing lighthearted adventures and wacky comedies most, he can't seem to turn down writing darker fiction. John lives with his wife, son, and Chihuahua.

Christopher P. Young

Chris grew up in the Maryland suburbs. He spent the majority of his childhood reading and writing science fiction and learning the craft of storytelling. He worked as a designer and producer in the video games industry for a number of years as well as working in technology and admin services. He enjoys writing both serious and comedic science fiction and fantasy. Chris lives with his wife and an ever-growing population of critters.

CRIMSON MYTH PRESS

Crimson Myth Press offers more books by this author as well as books from a few other hand-picked authors. From science fiction & fantasy to adventure & mystery, we bring the best stories for adults and kids alike.

www.CrimsonMyth.com

Printed in Great Britain
by Amazon